THE BOBBSEY TWINS
AND THE SECRET OF CANDY CASTLE

Candy Castle is made of sugar, lollipops, and mystery! The disappearance of the guard into its yawning black entrance and midnight lights in the peppermint tower set the scene for the Bobbseys' thrilling adventure.

"Watch out for spooks!" Skip Brewster, a new friend, warns. Then on the second day, when the twins are in charge of selling tickets for Tiny Town, the miniature buildings are wrecked!

Strange events follow. What happened to Mop, Skip's trick dog? And who knocked over the sand pirate?

The Bobbseys make startling discoveries which fans will not want to miss!

THE BOBBSEY TWINS BOOKS
By Laura Lee Hope

The
Bobbsey Twins
and the
Secret of
Candy Castle

By

LAURA LEE HOPE

GROSSET & DUNLAP

Publishers   New York

CONTENTS

CHAPTER I

SPOOK ISLAND

"HURRY!" exclaimed six-year-old Freddie Bobbsey. "Here comes the band!"

"Wait for me!" cried his blond twin, Flossie.

They raced off the excursion boat into Lakeport's new amusement park. Behind them came the twelve-year-old, dark-haired Bobbsey twins, Bert and Nan. They ran up to a wide avenue and found places in the front of the crowd.

"It's great!" exclaimed Bert as the redcoated musicians swung by, playing loudly.

Flossie glanced at a banner overhead and read aloud:

Opening Day
Happy Island

"Spook Island, you mean," said a tall, skinny red-haired boy.

On a leash he held a tiny black dog with very long hair. The animal pulled toward the passing musicians and barked.

1

BOOM! went the drums. With a wild yelp the dog broke loose and dashed among the marchers. A fat man blowing a tuba and looking at his music was only two rows behind. He did not see the animal.

"The dog will be stepped on!" Nan cried. "Here doggie!" she called.

Nan raised her hand and snapped her fingers. With a joyful bark the animal made a high leap toward her. He landed head first in the big, shiny tuba!

The drop knocked the instrument out of the player's mouth, but the man did not seem to know what had happened. He put the mouthpiece between his lips again, but the only sounds that came out were a dog's whines! By this time the crowd was laughing.

Nan ran after the man and caught his sleeve. "Wait a minute!" she cried. "There's a dog in your tuba!"

The musician stepped out of line as the red-haired boy came up. He reached down into the big brass horn and pulled out his pet.

"You okay, fella?" the boy asked. The dog wriggled in his master's arms and barked. "I'm very sorry," the boy said to the tuba player. "This little guy gets excited whenever he hears music."

The fat man rolled his eyes. "A dog! Well, nothing surprises me on this crazy island!" he exclaimed, and hurried off to catch up with the band. The Bobbseys wondered what he meant.

As the crowd began to break up, the other twins came over to Nan and the red-haired boy.

"Your dog's a swell jumper," said Freddie.

"He's a trained animal," his master replied proudly. "All you have to do is snap your fingers and up he goes! He's a sky diver, too."

"You mean that tiny little thing makes parachute jumps?" Nan asked, surprised.

"Yes."

"Oo, he's brave!" Flossie exclaimed.

"He likes to do it," the boy said.

"What's his name?" Nan asked.

"Mop."

"That's just what he looks like," said Nan.

She introduced herself and the other twins. "We live in Lakeport." She pointed across Lake Metoka to the town which was on the mainland.

The boy said his name was Skip Brewster. "My Dad's Flying Phil, the stunt pilot. He works here."

"We read about him," Bert spoke up. "He's going to give exhibitions, isn't he?"

"Yes, and take people for rides," Skip replied. "His plane is up on Flyaway Hill," he added and glanced at his watch. "I have to go there now. Mop's due to jump at three o'clock."

"From the plane?" Freddie asked.

"No, a high jumping board. Good-by."

"See you later," said Bert. "We work here, too."

"We have a special job," Freddie put in proudly, "but we don't have to do it till tonight."

"Tonight?" said Skip, widening his eyes. "Then watch out for spooks!" He hurried off with the dog under his arm.

"What did he mean by that?" Nan asked. "He didn't act as if he was kidding."

"And the tuba player called this a crazy island," Flossie spoke up.

"There must be some kind of mystery here," said Bert.

The twins' eyes sparkled with excitement. They loved mysteries and had solved a number of them.

"Let's ask Skip more about the spooks," Nan suggested.

"Okay, and I'll bet if we hurry we can see Mop jump," said Freddie.

The twins hastened into the amusement park and up a dirt road. It led from the dock to a wide avenue marked PROMENADE.

"Wow! Look at that!" exclaimed Freddie.

He pointed down the long street to a hill at the end of the island. On top of it was a round fairy-tale castle four stories high. It seemed to

be made of sparkling white sugar with a peppermint stick turret in the center and two other
towers in the shape of giant lollipops. A brisk
wind whipped banners on the turrets.

"It's a Candy Castle all right," said Bert. "A
fun house, too."

"When can we go in it?" Flossie asked.

"There'll be plenty of time later," Nan promised.

As the twins hurried down the midway, they
passed big noisy rides and colorful booths. At
the end of the avenue they took a chair lift
which carried them up Flyaway Hill.

At the top the Bobbseys found themselves on a
long, flat field. On the far side was the lake. A
red airplane stood in the middle of the field.

"That must be Mr. Brewster," Bert said.

At the edge of the hill was a small but high
springboard facing the field. A crowd waited
around it. Music blared from a loudspeaker as
Mop was being hoisted to the top of the board in
a basket.

The twins ran up to the platform just as the
dog trotted to the edge of it. He was wearing a
tiny flier's helmet. A loosely folded parachute
was attached to his back by a harness.

Skip stopped the record player and blew a
whistle. Eagerly the dog jumped off the
board.

"There he goes!" Freddie shouted.

The crowd applauded as the little parachute billowed out and Mop floated downward. Suddenly a hard gust of wind carried the tiny performer over the edge of the hill.

"He'll drop in the lake!" Nan cried.

A man next to her said, "If that dog gets tangled up in his parachute, he'll drown!"

Skip was already dashing down the steep slope. The Bobbseys ran after him.

"He's gone!" Skip called out wildly, not seeing his pet anywhere. "He could have blown away!"

"Fan out and search," Bert ordered. Quickly the others obeyed.

Halfway down the hill, Flossie heard shrill barking. Mop was hanging from the end of a thin tree branch. His parachute was caught, but as he struggled it kept ripping. He might drop into the lake any minute!

"Here he is! Hurry!" Flossie shouted. As Bert came running, the cloth tore again. "Oh, Mop, don't wiggle!" the little girl begged.

With a jump Bert caught a limb and swung himself up into the tree. He started to crawl out along the branch toward the trapped and shivering animal.

"No, Bert! It won't hold you," cried Nan as she ran up with the others.

Her brother stretched out carefully and reached for the dog. The limb bent and creaked loudly.

"The branch is breaking!"
cried Flossie

"The branch is breaking!" cried Flossie.

She clapped her hands over her eyes. Moments later she peeked through her fingers. Bert was inching back toward the trunk, clutching Mop and the parachute.

"That was great!" said Skip as Bert dropped to the ground and handed over the dog. "I don't know how to thank you."

"Has Mop ever blown away before?" Flossie asked.

"Yes, he has," Skip replied, "but never over a lake."

As they walked up the hill, he told the Bobbseys that every summer he and the dog traveled with his father to parks where the flier gave air shows. "My mother stays home in Virginia with my two little brothers."

"There's something I want to ask you," Bert said. "What did you mean about spooks on the island?"

"Of course I don't believe in ghosts," said Skip, "but there's something very creepy going on around here. One of the workmen told me about it. Every night this week after the watchman locked Candy Castle he saw a light moving around inside. He went to check, but there was never anybody there."

"Oo, that is spooky," said Flossie.

"There's more," Skip went on. "Some of the gimmicks in the castle are worked by pulleys with sandbags for weights. All of those bags were slashed open. And last week lots of tools were stolen from the equipment shed."

"It sounds as if somebody has it in for Mr. Flotow," said Bert.

"He's a friend of Daddy's," said Nan, "and since he's the owner of the island, he's letting us exhibit our Tiny Town here."

She explained that the children of Lakeport School had built a large model of a Western frontier town. "We'll charge admission and the money will go to the poor children of our sister town in New Zealand."

"It's named Lakeport, too," explained Flossie, "so that makes us sisters and we've agreed to do nice things for each other."

"Tiny Town opens tonight," said Freddie, "and we're going to sell tickets and be guides."

"Will you be doing that all summer?" Skip asked.

"Oh, no," said Bert. "We're just the first team." He explained that six groups of children had been picked to be in charge of the exhibit. "Three teams will take turns in July and the others in August."

"And somebody's mother or father will always be around in case we need 'em," put in Flossie.

"Dad's at Tiny Town now helping the men set

it up," Bert added as they reached the flying field.

After promising to see their new friend again, the twins left the hill and hurried to a clearing between the castle and the merry-go-round.

"Hi, Daddy!" called Flossie and raced up to a tall, handsome man who stood beside a cluster of small frame buildings.

"It looks wonderful," said Nan happily. The houses were about as high as she was.

"I had the men put sandbags under your mountains," he said. "They'll help hold up the framework."

The twins spent a busy evening at the exhibit. At closing time, a gong sounded.

Mr. Bobbsey walked over and said, "I'll take your cash box to Mr. Flotow's office. We're going home in his boat, so meet us at the dock in twenty minutes."

The twins covered the little town with a big green plastic sheet. By the time they reached the Promenade, the lights in the park were going out.

Suddenly from a side road came a short, stocky man with a flashlight. He had a big bunch of keys on his belt and wore a plaid cap.

"Mr. Kruger!" exclaimed Nan. It was their friend the janitor from Lakeport School.

"Well, if it isn't the Bobbseys!" he said.

"What are you doing here?" Bert asked him.

"I'm night watchman," said Mr. Kruger. "I—"

Nan gasped. "Look!" A light was moving in the dark castle!

"Come on!" Bert exclaimed. "Let's catch that spook!"

The twins raced up to the top of the hill with Mr. Kruger panting behind them. They stood aside as he unlocked the stout oaken door. Bert started into the dark passage.

"Wait!" said the watchman quickly. "I'll go."

He gave his cap a tug, set his jaw, and stepped inside. The twins watched his light go up the sloping passage and disappear around a corner.

They waited uneasily. Finally Nan called, "Mr. Kruger!" There was no answer. Then all four shouted together as loudly as they could. Still no answer.

"What happened to him?" Flossie whispered.

CHAPTER II

KING FREDDIE

"WE ought to go in and find Mr. Kruger," said Bert. He stepped into the dark fun house and felt for a light switch. There was none.

"If only we had a flashlight," said Nan.

"We'd better get Daddy and Mr. Flotow," Flossie piped up.

As she and Nan hurried down the hill, Freddie said, "Maybe Mr. Kruger went out the back door."

"If there is one," Bert said. "Let's look."

The brothers started to circle the tall castle, but stopped almost at once.

"It's too dark to see anything," said Bert. "We'd better wait for Dad."

Ten minutes later Mr. Bobbsey and the girls arrived with a small plump man puffing behind them. His bushy white hair was tousled and his pink face worried.

He trotted to the small ticket house in front of

12

the castle and unlocked the door. Stepping in, he flicked on a light. Then he inserted a thin key into a control panel on the wall. Instantly the castle was bathed in white floodlights. Bright colors glowed in the windows.

"Now," he said, "we'll see what happened to Kruger." He led the way inside the castle.

As the twins walked up the sloping passage, Flossie pointed to the walls. "They look as if they're covered with lemon drops."

The children turned a corner and entered a big room lit with pink light. Mr. Kruger was not there.

"Everything's made of make-believe candy!" exclaimed Freddie.

At one end stood a big wardrobe striped like peppermint. The other furniture seemed to be formed of twisted licorice whips.

The twins stared at a huge polished slide which came through a hole in the ceiling, swirled around the room and disappeared into an opening in the middle of the wall.

"Where does the slide go, Mr. Flotow?" asked Bert.

"It starts in the highest turret of the castle, passes through all the rooms and comes out in the courtyard."

"Maybe Mr. Kruger left that way," Nan put in.

The owner shook his head. "At night the

opening at the bottom is locked from the outside by a high iron fence. The watchman knows that."

Bert spotted a red-lighted exit sign over a door. "Maybe he went out there."

"No. The fire doors lock automatically inside and out at eleven o'clock. It's an electric system. They're set to open again at nine in the morning."

"How many rooms are in here?" Mr. Bobbsey asked.

"Four. One on each floor and one in the big tower."

What about the other turrets?" said Nan.

"They're just dummies. You can't go up in them."

Mr. Flotow led the Bobbseys into a hall, up a spiral stairway and into a brightly lit chamber on the second floor.

"It's a throne room!" exclaimed Nan.

A wide yellow carpet which seemed to be made of taffy led to a golden throne. Near it stood a large chest carved of maple sugar. Overhead was a sparkling chandelier of rock candy. The big slide cut across a corner of the room and went down through a hole in the floor. There was no sign of Mr. Kruger.

As the searchers walked into the hall, Freddie looked back longingly at the throne.

"I'd like to sit on that," he thought. Quick as a

wink, he hurried back and stepped onto the dais.

Pretending to be a king, Freddie seated himself on the huge chair. Instantly a metal band snapped around his waist. The throne sank through the floor!

"Help!" Freddie yelled as he dropped into the black pit!

The cry made the others turn back inside. Bert knelt at the side of the hole and looked down. "What happened?"

At once the throne zoomed up again. Bert ducked aside. The belt opened and snapped into the back of the chair.

As Freddie jumped up, the others reached him. "You okay, son?" asked Mr. Bobbsey.

"I'm all right," he said, but grinned sheepishly.

"That's one of our surprises," said Mr. Flotow. "All the gimmicks are electrical except the throne, which is set on springs and works when somebody sits on it."

Bert was still kneeling on the floor. His eye had caught something under the chest. He went over and pulled out a cap.

"That's Mr. Kruger's!" cried Nan.

"But it's torn now," said Flossie.

Bert handed the cap to Mr. Flotow. "Looks as if he was in a fight or an accident," said the park owner, and the others agreed.

They climbed up to the next floor, which was the royal bedchamber, and to the small room in the top of the turret where the slide began. There was no sign of the missing man.

"Shouldn't you notify the police, Mr. Flotow?" the twins' father asked.

"Perhaps."

Deeply worried, they filed down the long staircase and out of the castle and headed down the hill toward the dock.

Freddie suddenly said, "Maybe Mr. Kruger came out while Bert and I were away from the door."

"No," his brother replied. "We weren't gone long enough. Besides, he'd have called us."

"Maybe he thought you got tired of waiting," said the park owner.

"Mr. Kruger knows us better than that," said Nan.

But the little man liked the idea. "I'll bet that's just what happened," he said. "The cap was probably dropped by some workman."

The twins did not agree but said no more. When they reached the dock, Mr. Flotow led them to the far end where a large motorboat bobbed on the moonlit water.

They climbed aboard. He took the wheel and soon they were speeding toward the lights of Lakeport.

Then Nan spoke up. "We're detectives, Mr.

"Help!" Freddie shouted

Flotow," she said above the roar of the motor, "and we'd like to help you catch the castle spooks."

"Your father has told me about the mysteries you have solved," he replied. "I know you're very clever."

"We've always had good luck," said Bert modestly.

"I could certainly use help," declared Mr. Flotow, then added quickly, "but you must promise to be careful. I can't imagine who or what is behind the trouble."

"You can trust them to be sensible," said Mr. Bobbsey, and the twins grinned with pride.

"Good!" said Mr. Flotow. "Any time you twins want to go home in my boat, you come to the dock fifteen minutes after closing time. I'll take you right to your door in my car." The Bobbseys thanked him. "And don't worry about the watchman," he added. "He'll turn up." The twins hoped so.

Next morning they went to the park early. They met Mr. Flotow on the dock.

"Kruger's still missing," he told them. "He usually goes home on the first launch from here. It brings some workers over at seven o'clock and takes him back. They tell me he wasn't on the dock this morning. The police are here now, searching." He hurried off gloomily.

"I wonder if Skip knows about this," said Bert. "Let's go see him."

They found their red-haired friend on Flya-way Hill. He was talking to a tall man in khaki who looked just like him.

"This is my Dad," said Skip. As he intro-duced the Bobbseys, Mop frisked about them.

The flier gave the twins a little salute and grin. "I hear you rescued our dog," he said to Bert. "Whenever you feel like a free sky ride, let me know. That goes for all of you."

"Thanks, Mr. Brewster," said Bert and the others repeated it.

"Call me Phil," he replied smiling. "After all, we're co-workers."

But his smile faded as Bert told about the missing watchman.

"It sounds as if the prowlers in the castle kid-napped him," said the flier.

"But how did they get out?" Bert protested.

"I don't know," Phil admitted. "This spook stuff is dangerous. You be careful."

As he spoke, Nan noticed that Skip was hold-ing Mop's torn parachute.

"Why don't you give me that," she said, "and I'll sew it on Mother's machine."

Skip grinned. "That would be great," he said, handing it over. "I meant to fix the chute, but I'm not much good with a needle." Then he added, "Don't you have to work at Tiny Town?"

"Not till this afternoon," Nan replied. She explained that another team was on duty. "We came this morning to find out about Mr. Kruger. I'll take the parachute home now," she added.

"I have to get a new collar for Mop, too," said Skip, "so I'll go with you."

"Then you can stop at the motel, son," said Phil, "and pick up my watch. I forgot it this morning."

"We'll all go," said Bert.

The twins said good-by to Flying Phil and took the next launch across Lake Metoka. As they walked to the motel with Mop at their heels, Freddie said, "Guess what we have in our back yard, Skip. A rocket!"

The red-haired boy grinned. "Are you going to the moon?"

Bert laughed. "It's a car shaped like a rocket. Charlie Mason and I are going to be in the Air-Jet race this Saturday at the ball park." He explained that he and his best friend had built the car out of wood.

"It sounds keen," said Skip. "I'll come to see you race."

When they approached the motel, a thin man with slick black hair and a tiny mustache was coming out of the office. As he stepped off the stoop, he spotted them and stopped short.

"Young man," he called to Skip in a chilly voice, "come here!"

Skip walked over with Mop trotting beside him. The twins followed.

"I am the manager here," he said. "Last week while I was away, one of my employees permitted you to take a room, but dogs are not allowed." He added sharply. "You will have to leave."

"Oh please, no!" exclaimed Skip. "We had a hard time finding a place!"

The man hesitated and eyed Mop.

"He'll behave," Skip promised earnestly.

"We-ell, all right," said the manager. "But if he makes any trouble—out he goes, just like that!" He raised his hand and snapped his fingers. With a shrill bark, the tiny dog leaped high into the air and landed on the man's head.

With a yell the manager staggered backward. He stumbled against the stoop and sat down hard!

CHAPTER III

STOP THIEF!

AS the man landed on the motel step, the little dog jumped off his head. The children hurried to the motel manager's side.

"Are you hurt, sir?" Skip asked anxiously.

"Let us help you," said Nan, and Bert tried to take hold of his arm.

"Get back!" the man said angrily, "and keep that animal away from me."

As Flossie scooped up Mop, the manager, pale and tight-lipped, struggled to his feet. "That dog must be out of here by six o'clock tonight!" he said firmly, and stalked into his office. He slammed the door.

"Oh, Mop, how could you?" said Nan to the dog.

"It wasn't his fault," said Flossie. "He thought the man was signaling him to jump."

"We're really in the soup now," said Skip gloomily. "We may not be able to find another place to stay. Not many motels will take dogs and, besides, Lakeport is crowded with summer visitors."

"You mean you and Mop'll have to go home?" Freddie asked anxiously.

"I sure hope not," said Skip, "but I don't know—"

"Something may turn up," said Nan kindly. "Go get your father's watch. Then we'll take your parachute to our house."

Skip went to his room to do the errand. A few minutes later the five children started down the street with Mop trotting at their heels. The twins tried to be cheerful, but all of them were downcast at the thought of losing their new friend.

When they reached the front yard, the Bobbseys found their mother on her knees weeding a flower bed. She stood up and dusted off her blue slacks.

"Hello," she said, smiling. Mrs. Bobbsey was a pretty, slender young woman with a sweet face. "I didn't expect you home this noon. Did something go wrong?"

Bert introduced Skip and his dog. Mrs. Bobbsey picked up Mop. As she petted him, Nan showed her the parachute.

"It can be mended easily," said her mother, then glanced keenly at their faces. "Now let's all go in and have lunch," she added, "and you can tell me what's the matter."

Flossie whispered to Skip, "Mother always knows when there's trouble."

"My Mom's like that too," said Skip.

Just then a large, shaggy white dog came trotting around the corner of the house followed by a fox terrier. Instantly Mop ran forward yapping shrilly. The other two dogs barked loudly.

"Hold it, Waggo!" exclaimed Bert, catching the terrier's collar.

"Quiet, Snap!" said Nan, going to the big dog.

Skip picked up Mop. "Now you cut it out and be friends."

Freddie told Skip that Snap was a trick dog too. "We solved a mystery about a circus one time. That's where we found him."

"We 'dopted him," said Flossie. "And there is Snoop." She pointed to the porch rail where a large black-and-white cat was sitting.

Mrs. Bobbsey called the children and they trooped into the house followed by the animals. After freshening up, they sat down at the big kitchen table. Skip was introduced to Dinah, the jolly woman who had helped with the cooking and housekeeping since Bert and Nan were born. Dinah passed a platter of sandwiches and poured foaming milk shakes.

"I'll give that little dog of yours a drink," she said to Skip with a big smile. She set out a bowl of cool water.

Nan explained to Skip that Dinah's husband, Sam Johnson, worked in Mr. Bobbsey's lumberyard on Lake Metoka. They lived on the third floor of the house.

During lunch Bert told his mother about the missing watchman. She looked grave.

Then Nan reported what had happened at the motel. "If Skip can't stay, we're all going to miss a lot of fun."

While listening, Mrs. Bobbsey had quietly watched the visitor. "There's no problem," she said with a smile, "if Mr. Brewster will allow Skip and Mop to stay with us the rest of the summer."

"Oh Mommy, that's super!" cried Flossie.

The older twins beamed, and Skip flushed to the roots of his hair. "That would be wonderful," he said. "Could we really?"

"Of course," said Mrs. Bobbsey. "When lunch is over, I will write a note to your father and you can take it to him."

Later, as the children were leaving with Mop, Mrs. Bobbsey said to the twins, "Your father has some business with Mr. Flotow, so he will be at the island this afternoon. I'll be over tonight and we'll have supper there."

"So we can all eat together!" said Flossie happily.

Before leaving, Bert attached a flashlight to his belt. "From now on, I'm taking this," he said.

Half an hour later Nan was seated at a small ticket table in front of Tiny Town. Flossie and Bert were showing people through the miniature streets.

A short time afterward, a handsome gray-haired man in a tan suit came up and bought a ticket. When he entered Tiny Town, Nan noticed he carried a cane with a large gold knob for a handle.

"Tell me, young man," he said to Freddie, "what are these buildings made of?"

"Wood," replied the boy. Taking a deep breath, he began to tell the story of how the children of his school had made the town.

"Never mind all that," said the man quickly. "What about the mountains?"

"We stretched burlap on a wooden frame and squirted on some plastic stuff to make it stiff," Freddie explained. "After that, we painted it to look like rocks. There are sandbags underneath," he added.

"Ah, is that so?" the man said mildly. "Thank you, young man." He walked away and Freddie turned to go.

Suddenly the boy heard a beeping noise behind him. He looked back. The man quickly put his hand over the gold knob on the cane and the sound stopped. Freddie stared at him, but the man smiled, nodded and left the exhibit.

Puzzled, Freddie went back to Nan. "That

man who was just in here—his cane was beeping."

"Was what?" Nan asked.

Before her brother could explain, a short young man with brown curly hair came up. He was wearing a wrinkled white suit with a pink plastic flower in his buttonhole.

"Look!" he suddenly exclaimed, pointing to Tiny Town. As Nan and Freddie turned around, he snatched the cash box and ran.

"Stop thief!" Nan cried and Freddie shouted, "Catch him!"

They dashed after the fleeing man. Bert, Flossie, and their customers followed. But the fellow disappeared among the rides on the Promenade.

"What happened? What's the matter!" cried Mr. Flotow, as he and Mr. Bobbsey came hurrying toward Bert.

Behind them were two park policemen. Curious onlookers gathered around as Nan told what had happened.

Freddie was just coming back. "Here's the cash box," he said. "I found it by the merry-go-round. But it's empty."

"That's nothing!" called a man. "I had my pocket picked here this afternoon."

"And my purse was snatched," cried a woman. "A short, curly-haired man did it!"

"Please, folks," said Mr. Flotow loudly, "we'll do our best to catch the thieves!"

As the crowd melted away, he groaned. "What next? I've had other complaints about a pickpocket with curly hair. It's the same fellow, I'll bet. Besides, business is terrible since Kruger disappeared. People have been scared off."

Just then Mrs. Bobbsey arrived. She was shocked at the story. For the rest of the afternoon she sat beside the ticket table. At six o'clock the twins turned over the cash box to the new team, Nellie Parks, Tara O'Toole, Charlie Mason, and Ralph Blake. Mr. Mason was with them. Bert told them about the theft.

"We'll be very careful," said Nellie, who was Nan's best friend. She was a pretty girl with dark blond hair.

Charlie, a good-looking boy, was Bert's closest friend. "Ralph and I'll stay with the cash box," he said. "The girls can be guides."

"And I'll stick close by," Charlie's father promised.

At supper in the cafeteria Mrs. Bobbsey told her husband about Skip coming to stay at their house.

"Good idea," he said.

After eating, the children's parents took a walk, while the twins went to Candy Castle. When they reached the low stone wall that went all the way around the courtyard, they stopped to look.

"Oo, it's bee-yoo-ti-ful!" Flossie exclaimed.

"Stop thief!" called Nan

Freddie grinned. "That's a neat slide coming out of the wall. It's—oh!"

At that moment something came tumbling head over heels from the slide. All the twins could see was a mass of bright colors. Then it stood up. A clown!

"D-did you hurt yourself?" Flossie called to him.

"No," said the clown, laughing. He walked over and patted her blond curls. "I do this to amuse the children who come here. Did you like it?"

"Oh, yes!" the twins cried.

"Come, I'll take you inside," the clown said. "I'm also one of the guards."

The Bobbseys followed. Bert whispered, "Keep your eyes open for clues."

They hurried up the passage and into the first room. Children screamed as they slid through the hole in the ceiling and out the opening in the wall.

Freddie gave a yelp. "The floor's tipping!"

Laughing, the twins wobbled on what looked like bubbling fudge. On the second floor a yellow "taffy" carpet pulled back and forth under their feet. Each child sat on the sinking throne. Flossie giggled at the hard cushion which looked like a big piece of chocolate candy.

"I want to zip down the slide!" Freddie called.

The twins hurried up to the next floor and rode in a swinging bed. Then they went to the tower. By the time they reached the top of the slide Freddie and Flossie were not sure they wanted to go down.

"Don't be afraid," said the attendant, a young man with a friendly grin. He took a burlap bag from a box beside him and put it at the top of the slide. "Sit on that, fold your arms and keep your feet together."

"Okay, I'll go first," said Nan. She sat down, gave a little squeak and zipped out of sight. The others followed. Faster and faster they slid on the highly polished wood. Down through the rooms they swooped, sped through a dark narrow tunnel and shot out into a pit of foam rubber which looked like a bed of marshmallows.

Spectators stood around laughing and pointing as the children bounced to a stop. An attendant helped them out of the courtyard and collected the bags.

"There's Mommy—and Daddy too!" said Flossie.

"It was great, Dad!" said Freddie as the children joined their parents.

"A real thrill ride," Bert agreed, but he could not help remembering that Mr. Kruger had disappeared in this house of fun.

"We didn't find a single clue," thought Nan. Then the family went to Flyaway Hill. Bert introduced his mother and father to Flying Phil. The flier's keen blue eyes quickly looked the couple over. Then he smiled.

"I think you folks are terrific to invite Skip and Mop to your house. I'd be mighty pleased to have them stay with you."

All the children beamed, and Flossie clapped her hands for joy.

"It's settled then," said Mr. Bobbsey cheerfully, tousling Skip's hair. "We'll pick up his clothes on the way home."

That night Skip slept on a comfortable cot in the Bobbsey boys' room. Mop curled up at his feet.

Next morning the five children reached the park before it was open to the public. Skip headed for Flyaway Hill with Mop under his arm. The twins hurried to Tiny Town. As it came into view Nan cried out in dismay.

"It's been smashed!"

CHAPTER IV

A MEAN TRICK

THE children raced forward to look at their damaged exhibit.

"Just the mountain end is gone," said Bert. The big green plastic cover still lay over the rest of the miniature buildings.

"But that's a lot," said Nan. "Who would do such an awful thing?"

"The schoolhouse is smashed and the stable, too," cried Flossie. "The poor horses are broken."

"Look at this," said Freddie. He held up a headless cowboy.

"The mountains are entirely wrecked," Bert remarked.

The plastic form of the rocks had been hacked apart and the sandbags beneath had been slit open. Some of the sand had been dumped on the fragile buildings. Helplessly the children stared at the ruin.

"No use standing around and looking at it," Bert said grimly. "We'd better get to town for repair supplies."

"We'll never be able to open for business today," said Freddie. "It's going to take a long time to fix all this."

"Maybe Skip can help us," Bert suggested. "You three go ask him. I'll report this to Mr. Flotow."

The girls hurried to Flyaway Hill with Freddie. They found Skip with his father washing the plane while Mop watched.

"Hi! What's up?" Skip asked when he saw them running toward him.

Quickly the children told what had happened. The flier looked serious and Skip shook his head.

"More spook trouble," said Skip. "I wonder what it's all about."

"Who knows?" said Flying Phil. "Son, you run along and help the Bobbseys. They need you more than I do."

"Okay," said Skip. He picked up his dog. "I'll go to town with you and buy a collar for Mop. It slipped my mind after the excitement at the motel yesterday."

The four met Bert on the dock and caught the next launch back to Lakeport.

"Mr. Flotow was pretty upset," said Bert. "He sent for the police again."

Freddie looked puzzled. "How could he do that? There's no telephone on the island."

"No, but he radios to the Happy Island Ticket Office on the mainland dock, and they do the telephoning," Bert replied. "I have an idea on how to catch the prowlers," he added.

"How?" the others asked eagerly.

"By leaving the slide exit of the castle open and secretly putting an electric eye there. Then if the troublemakers try to leave that way, they'll set off the electric alarm. It'll be heard all over the island. Maybe the new watchman can catch them."

"Is Mr. Flotow going to do it?" Nan asked.

"Yes," her twin replied.

After the launch docked, the five walked quickly to the hardware store where Bert bought the repair materials.

Meanwhile Skip looked around for a collar to fit Mop. "They don't have any small enough," he told Nan.

"There's a pet shop on the next block," she said. "We'll try there."

The clerk handed Bert his purchases in one big bundle and the children left the hardware store. On the corner Freddie paused in front of the Goody Shoppe.

"Let's get ice cream cones," he suggested.

The children entered the shop with the little dog at their heels.

"Are you going to get one for Mop?" Flossie asked Skip.

"Sure. He likes vanilla."

"Let me feed it to him," Flossie begged.

"Me, too," Freddie put in.

Skip grinned. "You can take turns."

When the cones were ready, the children went outside. They stood close to the window and licked their ice cream. Flossie stooped beside Mop and held his cone for him while she ate her own.

They had almost finished eating, when Nan glanced up the street and saw a small old man coming toward them. He had silky white hair and eyebrows.

"He's frail looking," Nan thought, seeing how feebly he was walking.

Suddenly the wail of a siren split the air. At once the children looked down the street in the opposite direction.

"Here come the police!" cried Freddie.

"I wonder what happened?" Bert said as they all stepped to the curb to look after the squad car.

"Should we go see?" asked Freddie. "Mop's through with his ice cream."

"No. We ought to get back to Tiny Town," said Nan.

Turning around, the children were surprised to see the old man stooping beside Mop. He seemed to be feeling the long hair around the dog's neck.

When the children walked over, he looked up and smiled. "Just petting the dear little dog," he said in a high shaky voice. He put his hand against the wall of the Goody Shoppe and tried to rise.

"May I help you?" Bert said quickly. He put out his hand and steadied the old man as he got to his feet.

"Thank you," he said. "What is your name?"

As he asked the question, Bert noticed what bright blue eyes he had. "He may be feeble, but he's pretty sharp," the boy thought. He answered the man's question politely.

"I assume this fine little dog belongs to you," the old man said.

Skip spoke up. "No, sir. He's mine."

The bright blue eyes fixed themselves on Skip. "And where do you live, young man?" he asked.

"He's staying with us," Freddie said quickly.

The old man smiled, said good-by, and walked slowly around the corner. The next moment there came a loud OOGA-OOGA!

"Get out of the way!" shouted a voice.

The children whirled to see two boys speeding toward them on bicycles. As the twins and Skip leaped aside, the riders swerved into the street. They circled around, bounced over the curb and came back.

"Ha-ha-ha!" said the first one. "Scared you, didn't we?"

The twins looked disgusted. Danny Rugg and his pal, Jack Westley liked to make trouble for the Bobbseys whenever they could. Danny was a big boy, about Bert's age, and Jack was just a little shorter. Their favorite fun was picking on smaller children.

The bullies dismounted and stood astride their bikes. Jack eyed Mop. "Look at that," he said with a grin.

Danny stared at the dog and smirked. "What is it?" he asked. "A rat?"

"Course not!" Flossie said indignantly. "He's a trick dog!"

Danny turned to Bert. "Fourth of July's coming soon. I'll bet you haven't got any firecrackers yet."

"No, we haven't," Bert replied. "You know they're against the law in Lakeport."

Jack snickered. "We know a roadside stand outside of town where you can get 'em."

"But we're not telling you," said Danny.

"We're not interested," said Nan. "There'll be plenty of fireworks at Happy Island on the Fourth of July."

The bullies looked at each other and grinned. Then they got onto their bikes and pedaled around the corner, laughing.

"Who are those two?" Skip asked.

Bert explained. A moment later they heard a snicker. Danny was peering around the corner of the shop. Suddenly he hurled a firecracker toward Mop.

BANG!

As the children jumped back, the dog gave a yelp and shot off down the street.

"Mop!" cried Skip. "Come here!" He dashed after the dog.

Quickly Bert thrust the parcel into Nan's arms and raced after Skip. Freddie ran behind the two other boys.

At the same time the old man hobbled quickly around the corner. "The dog!" he gasped. He started to run but Nan caught his arm.

"No, no! You'll fall!"

"But the dog!" he cried, his eyes wide with alarm. "Catch him!"

"Don't worry. The boys will do it," Nan said.

The man put his hand over his eyes and shook his head miserably. Nan took his arm.

"Come inside the Goody Shoppe," she said. He allowed the girls to lead him in and seat him at a table.

Looking worried, the woman clerk brought a glass of water. He drank a sip and assured them that he would be all right.

As the woman returned to the counter, Nan said, "You really ought not to upset yourself this way."

BANG!

"I know," he quavered, "but I'm very fond of dogs. I'm so afraid the little fellow will get run over."

At that moment the boys were fearing the same thing. They had chased the frightened dog down the avenue and seen him dash blindly across two side streets.

"He's like lightning!" Bert panted, dodging passersby. Several people turned to stare when the tiny black ball of fur shot past. At the end of the street was a large intersection, busy with traffic.

"If he crosses that street on a red light, he'll get hit!" Skip thought.

The next moment the dog reached the corner and dashed into the stream of cars. Brakes screeched. Drivers shouted. Somehow the panic-stricken animal managed to get across unharmed. By the time the boys reached the opposite side, Mop was almost to the end of the next block.

Suddenly three little girls on roller skates came around the corner and coasted toward the fleeing dog. He swerved to the curb where a delivery truck was parked with the back doors open.

Mop gave a high leap and sailed inside it. An instant later a man in gray shirt and trousers walked out of the store, carrying a large empty metal tray. He slid it into the back of the truck and slammed the doors.

"Now we can get him!" Freddie cried.

Shouting at the driver, the boys ran harder. But the man did not look back. He swung himself up behind the wheel and drove off.

CHAPTER V

FLYING SAUCERS

"WAIT!" Skip yelled. "My dog's inside your truck!"

The driver paid no attention. He turned the corner and disappeared. Panting, the boys stopped running.

"Poor Mop! We almost had him!" Freddie sighed.

"We'll find him," said Bert. "That truck belongs to the Bonny Bread Company. I'll call them up and find out where it's going."

He fished a coin out of his pocket and ran to a phone booth in the middle of the block. Finally he came out.

"The truck is on its way to the Daisy Delicatessen. That's about two blocks from here."

"But the truck'll be gone by now," Skip cut in.

"I know," said Bert, "but the next stop is a supermarket over at the shopping center. Maybe we can catch it there."

Once again the three set out on a run. As they reached the center, the boys saw the truck pull into the parking lot. They raced up to the driver when he jumped down to the pavement. Quickly Bert explained the problem.

The driver shoved his cap back and cocked his head. "A dog in my truck!" he exclaimed. "Well, let's have a look."

He led the way to the back. The boys heaved sighs of relief. They clustered around the driver as he opened the double doors. Wide shelves of bread lined the trays inside.

Mop was not in sight!

Skip whistled, but his pet did not appear.

"You're little," said the driver to Freddie. "Go in and take a look."

Freddie climbed into the truck and searched carefully among the trays of bread and in the corners. Mop was not there.

"He must have jumped out when you made your other stop," said Bert to the driver.

"I guess so," the man replied. "Sorry."

The boys thanked him and turned away, discouraged. "What now?" Freddie asked.

"We'd better hurry back to the Daisy Delicatessen," said Skip. "Mop might be hanging around there."

They searched there for an hour but failed to locate the dog.

"Mop's so little, it's easy to miss him," Skip remarked gloomily. "And what makes it worse, he has no collar on to identify him."

Bert nodded. "Besides, there's no telling where he is by now. We may as well go home."

When the boys arrived they found the girls in the kitchen with their mother and Dinah. There was a gingery smell of baking cookies, but the downcast boys hardly noticed.

"Where's Mop?" Flossie asked, hopping off a stool.

Bert shook his head, and the tired boys sat down at the table. As they told their story, the others listened quietly.

"I know how you feel," said Mrs. Bobbsey, patting Skip's shoulder. "But we won't give up. Let's put an ad in the paper and offer a reward."

"Somebody'll find that little old dog," said Dinah cheerfully. "Don't you worry."

Just then the back door opened and a thin, friendly looking colored man came in.

"Sam," Dinah said to him, "we got bad news." She told him what had happened. "I'd like to give that Danny Rugg a piece of my mind!" she added hotly.

"That won't do any good now," said Sam quietly. "We need to get word around for everybody to look for Mop."

"Oh, Sam, that gives me an idea!" Nan exclaimed. "Maybe we can have an announcement made on TV. After all, Mop isn't just an ordinary dog. He's a special performer."

Mrs. Bobbsey agreed. "You make the calls, Bert, while we get lunch ready."

When her son returned to the kitchen ten minutes later, he looked more cheerful. "The TV station said yes, and the *Lakeport Times* will run an ad in tonight's paper."

Flossie spoke up. "Remember the old man downtown? He was very worried about Mop. Maybe he'll see him."

Bert looked thoughtful. "Why should he care so much about Mop?"

"You mean," said Nan, "that if he finds him he might not give him up?"

"Maybe." Bert now told his mother his scheme to catch the spook.

"It might work," she agreed.

"It's keen," said Freddie. "I can just see that old spook shooting out of the slide and there you are waiting in the courtyard. And you've got him—ha ha!"

Skip managed to smile. "Or he's got you!"

"I didn't think of that," said Freddie. Flossie giggled.

Nan glanced at the kitchen clock. "It's almost noon!" she exclaimed. "Let's listen to the newscast. Maybe they'll tell about Mop!"

She hurried to the living room and turned on the television set. The others, including Dinah and Sam, followed her and all listened carefully to the newscaster. The big story of the day was that a ruby pendant had been stolen from Bender's Jewelry Store in Lakeport two hours before.

"That's when we heard the sirens," said Bert. "I'll bet they were on their way to Bender's."

"Shh!" Nan said. "Listen!"

The announcer was telling about Mop. He asked anyone who had seen him to call the Bobbseys' house or the Happy Island office on the mainland dock. He gave telephone numbers for both places.

"That reminds me," said Bert as Nan turned off the set, "I'd better call Charlie and tell him what happened at Tiny Town. His team can help fix the damage."

After lunch Nan picked up the parcel of repair supplies from the hall. "Let's hurry," she urged.

Mrs. Bobbsey took a neatly wrapped package from the table. "Here is Mop's parachute," she said to Skip. "Nan has been so busy that I sewed it."

The boy looked sad as he thanked her. Seeing the children's worried faces, Mrs. Bobbsey took her purse from the table. "You all need a little treat to help you forget your troubles," she said.

"Why don't you have supper at the park and spend the evening going on the rides?" She handed Bert some money.

"You're terrific, Mommy!" exclaimed Freddie, hugging her as the other children said thanks.

"Daddy has business again at the island this afternoon," the twins' mother went on. "He plans to stay over for the evening, so you can come home with him in Mr. Flotow's motorboat."

The children hurried to the park. After Skip told his father about Mop, he joined the repair crew at Tiny Town.

By late afternoon Bert looked over their progress. "We've nearly finished," he announced.

Charlie kept whistling as he painted rocks. "This is fun," he said.

Flossie gave a loud sigh. "I'm tired of gluing these broken horses," she complained.

"Me too," said Freddie. "I'm all stuck up."

"Why don't you take a rest?" said Nan. "Go on some of the rides. Here's the money."

With sighs of relief the young twins hurried to the Promenade. Right away Freddie bought a huge red balloon on a stick. At the same stand Flossie got a straw hat with a big brim.

As she put it on, her twin said, "Let's go on the Flying Saucers!" They looked up at the silver-colored discs which flew around a big pole on cables.

The twins ran to the booth and bought tickets. Two minutes later the saucers stopped twirling and settled down to a platform. The riders trooped off and the waiting customers went up the ramp to the loading gate. The young twins sat together in one of the spacecraft and fastened their seat belts.

"Don't you think you'd better leave that balloon with me?" the attendant asked Freddie.

"No, thanks. I'll keep it," the little boy said, gripping the stick tightly.

A moment later the saucer began to whirl, going higher and higher. The wind whipped the children's faces and suddenly lifted Flossie's hat.

"Help!" she screeched, grabbing for it. As Freddie caught her hat, the wind tore the balloon from his hand. He made a wild grab for it, but was too late.

"My balloon!" he cried. As the twins rode round and round, they tried to keep track of the huge red toy. It drifted downward.

"Lucky it's not filled with gas," said Flossie, "or it would have blown away."

When the ride was over, the twins dashed down the ramp. They could see the balloon drifting along a side street. The wind blew

"My balloon!" he cried

harder and rolled the balloon around the roller coaster. The twins hurried to the back of the huge structure. Before them was a large empty field with bushes here and there. The balloon was not in sight.

A workman was sitting on the ground nearby, leaning against the roller coaster. He had a pipe but instead of holding it in his mouth, he had the bowl of it against his ear. The twins thought this very strange. He did not notice them coming toward him.

"Excuse me," said Freddie. "Did you see—?"

Startled, the man looked up. He dropped the pipe. When Freddie stooped to pick it up, the man snatched the pipe away.

"What're you kids doing here? Get out!" he growled.

CHAPTER VI

THE MIDNIGHT SHADOW

FREDDIE and Flossie stared at the rude man.

"I was only going to ask you—I didn't mean to—" Freddie started to say. His voice faded out as the workman's hard black eyes bored into his.

The fellow had coarse, black crew-cut hair and wore a blue shirt and coveralls. Big muscles bulged under his rolled-up sleeves.

Flossie clutched Freddie's arm. "There's your balloon!" she said and pointed across the field. The red balloon had blown from behind a bush.

The children ran over, and Freddie caught it. When they turned back toward the roller coaster, the man was gone.

Flossie frowned. "He was mean."

"He was acting funny, too," said Freddie. "I wonder why he had that pipe up to his ear."

When they got to Tiny Town, the twins told the others about the stranger.

Nan smiled. "You've had an exciting two days, Freddie. First you meet a man with a beeping cane, now you see a fellow who listens to his pipe!"

"You're doing great, boy!" said Bert with a chuckle. He tousled his brother's hair and started to pack up the paint cans and brushes.

Nan gave a sigh of relief. "It's all fixed now," she said, looking around Tiny Town. Jack and Charlie were putting the tools in a bag.

"We lost a day," Nellie remarked, "but everything's shipshape for the number three team tonight."

Tara spoke up with a grin. "That's the biggest balloon I ever saw, Freddie. Are you carrying it or is it carrying you?"

The little boy grinned. "I can handle it. See?"

He spun around, and the balloon hit the saw in Charlie's hand. BANG!

"Aw-w, nuts!" said Freddie, looking at the limp pieces of rubber.

"Too bad," said Nan kindly. "We'll get another one sometime."

The Bobbseys and Skip said good-by to the other team. Then they carried the leftover supplies to the Administration Building, which looked like a big blue mushroom. The children knocked on Mr. Flotow's office door.

"Come in!" he called.

As they entered, Mr. Bobbsey looked up, surprised. "I see I'm going to have company for dinner," he said with a grin.

"Put your supplies over in the corner, children," Mr. Flotow told them. "I'll lock everything in the cupboard later on." The twins stacked the boxes against the wall.

"Come see what Mr. Flotow's planning," said the twins' father. He pointed to a large colored drawing which lay on the park owner's desk. The children gathered around curiously.

"It's a swimming pool!" Flossie exclaimed.

"With a big wooden bathing pavilion next to it," said Bert.

His father nodded. "That's where the Bobbsey lumberyard comes in," he said.

"When are you going to build the pool and where's it going to be?" Freddie asked eagerly.

"I want to put the pool in that big meadow behind the roller coaster," said Mr. Flotow. "But ever since Mr. Kruger disappeared, business has been getting worse and worse. I'm afraid to go ahead with the project."

"We heard from the police a little while ago," said Mr. Bobbsey, "and so far they haven't found a single clue to the missing watchman."

"The answer to the whole mystery is in the castle, I'm sure," said Bert.

Mr. Flotow nodded. "Maybe your idea will

work, Bert. I had the electric eye put near the bottom of the slide. The new night watchman has been ordered to hurry to the courtyard the minute he sees the light in the castle."

"It's worth trying anyway," said Mr. Bobbsey.

After supper, while the men went over plans for the pool, the twins and Skip enjoyed the rides. All too soon the closing gong rang.

"We don't have to meet Daddy and Mr. Flotow at the dock for almost half an hour," said Nan. "Let's take a look around the castle."

By the time they reached the foot of the hill the wooden sidewalk leading to the summit had stopped running. The castle itself was dark.

Suddenly Nan seized Bert's arm and pointed. There was a light in a first-floor window!

"Come on!" said Bert. "Quick!"

He hurried up the walk with the others close behind. The light vanished. Before long it showed in a higher window, then one higher still.

"Someone's climbing the stairs!" Nan said.

As they reached the castle, the light appeared in the top of the turret. The five children raced into the courtyard. Suddenly the light in the tower went out, but began to whip past the window on the other floors.

"Somebody's on the slide!" Nan cried.

"The minute he hits that foam rubber, I'll turn the flashlight on him and you all yell," Bert said tensely.

The children stood anxiously watching the dark mouth of the slide. Bert held his flashlight ready. Moments ticked by.

Suddenly there was a faint clicking noise. Instantly Bert switched on the beam. Would the spook be on the slide? Only a thin white pen rolled out of the slide.

The children held their breaths. Time went by. No one appeared!

"How about that?" Skip asked softly.

"It sure is strange," said Bert. Taking a handkerchief from his pocket, he picked up the pen with it.

"There might be fingerprints," he remarked. On the side of the pen were the words, *Courtesy of Melrose Bank*.

"But who dropped it?" Freddie asked. "And where is he?"

"That's what I'd like to know," said his brother. "Once you're on that slide there's no getting off."

Just then Mr. Bobbsey, Mr. Flotow and a thin man with a flashlight ran around the corner of the castle.

"Did you get him, Bert?" cried the park owner.

Bert explained, and gave Mr. Flotow the pen

Would the spook be on the slide?

in the handkerchief. The thin man, who was introduced as the new watchman, looked worried.

Grim-faced, Mr. Flotow opened the castle and turned on the lights. Once again the three men and the children searched the fantastic building. It was empty.

"There has to be a secret exit," said Bert as they all gathered outside again.

"Can't be!" said the park owner positively. "The castle is an entirely new building. I drew the plans myself."

"Does it have a cellar?" Nan asked.

"No," the owner replied. "We didn't need one since the place doesn't have to be heated." Then he added quickly, "Wait a minute! I forgot! There *is* a cellar, but there's no way to reach it."

The children looked puzzled. "What do you mean?" Freddie asked.

"There used to be a house on this spot. But it was in ruins, so I tore it down when I bought the island last March. The foundations were solid, though, and I built the castle right on top of them."

Mr. Bobbsey said, "This used to be the summer home of a wealthy family named Webb. They had everything here—a boathouse, tennis courts, and a beach. But the place had been deserted for ten years," he added. "When the Webbs stopped coming it fell into ruins."

"Maybe there's an exit from the cellar," Bert suggested.

"No, my boy, I'm sorry," said Mr. Flotow. "That cellar is nine feet deep with solid stone walls. Even if there were a way out, there's no way *into* it from the castle."

"So that's that," said Mr. Bobbsey.

The park owner ordered the watchman to stay around the fun house until morning. It was midnight now.

Ten minutes later, the others were cutting across the lake in Mr. Flotow's powerful boat. They looked back at the island. The shoreline was dark.

Suddenly Nan exclaimed, "There's a light!" She pointed to a wavering beam at the foot of the hill. The beam moved along the beach and disappeared around one end of the island.

"That's funny," said Mr. Flotow. "This boat was the last to leave. There's not supposed to be anyone left over there except the watchman."

Bert spoke up. "I have a hunch, Mr. Flotow. Could you cut off your engine for a few minutes?"

The park owner turned the key, and the sound of the motor died. "What is it?" he asked.

"Let's just listen for a minute."

Drifting in the darkness, they strained their ears. At first there was silence. Then in the distance they could hear the *chug-chug* of another boat. It was coming toward them!

"It's running without lights," Skip whispered.

Bert was excited. "Now's our chance to see who it is!" he whispered. "When he gets close, let's turn the light on him!"

"That's too risky," Mr. Bobbsey said. "We must get you children to safety before we try any detective work. Whoever is behind this mystery could be dangerous."

Mr. Flotow turned on the lights and piloted his launch toward the dock on the mainland. The other boat followed.

"Why is he trailing us?" Nan asked. "I should think he'd be sneaking away, if he doesn't want to be seen."

"I don't know," said Mr. Flotow grimly, "but the fellow's not going to catch us!" He put on speed and the big craft roared away.

At the dock they waited for the mysterious person to arrive. But no boat came.

"I guess he changed his mind and docked somewhere else," Mr. Bobbsey said. "There's no use in our waiting."

Mr. Flotow said he would stay around for a while, so the Bobbseys called a taxi and went home. The twins' mother had been worried by the long absence and hustled Freddie and Flossie off to bed at once.

Before going upstairs Bert said, "I wish we could go to Melrose tomorrow and check at the bank on that pen we found."

"I'll take you," his father offered. "I have business there."

Just then there came a loud sneeze just outside the window where they were standing.

"Somebody's spying on us!" Skip cried.

CHAPTER VII

A HIDDEN BOAT

QUICKLY Bert beckoned to Skip, Nan and his father, then led the way outside. Cautiously they peered over the row of bushes which grew along the front of the house. No one was there!

Using his flashlight, Bert examined the ground under the window. He pointed out two small shoe prints.

"He must have been a little man," Skip remarked.

"The man who stole the Tiny Town cash box was small," Nan remembered. "Do you think he was the same one?"

"Could be," said Bert. "And maybe he's the castle spook too."

"I think there's more than one man," Skip remarked. "It must have taken at least two to kidnap Mr. Kruger."

Mrs. Bobbsey had come downstairs and heard

the whole story. "It's my opinion," she said, "that several men are responsible for the mystery. They're curious about your next move."

"That's right," said the twins' father. "You will have to be very careful tomorrow in Melrose. The eavesdropper may have heard our plans.

"Now run along to bed and I'll report this to the police. You three and I," he whispered, "will go to Melrose about noon."

"What about Tiny Town?" Skip asked the twins. "Don't you have to work?"

"No," Nan replied. "We have tomorrow and the next day off because we were there three days."

Next morning when the twins came down to brunch, Skip was missing.

"I guess he's still asleep," said Nan. "His door's closed."

"No," her mother replied, placing a platter of hot pancakes on the table. "We had a phone call this morning from a woman who thinks she has found Mop. Skip has gone to see her."

"Oh, I hope it *is* Mop!" said Nan.

"I wish Freddie and I were going to Melrose," Flossie spoke up, pouring lots of syrup on her pancakes.

"Some other time, my little fat fairy," said Mr. Bobbsey. Flossie always smiled when he used his special pet name for her.

"You, too, my little fireman," he said to Freddie. Mr. Bobbsey had given his son this nickname because Freddie loved fire engines and wanted to be a fireman when he grew up.

"You two can work on the rocket car," said Bert. "Charlie's coming over this afternoon. We were going to paint it, but I won't be here, so you can help him." This pleased the small twins.

Half an hour later Mr. Bobbsey backed the station wagon out of the drive with the older twins beside him. "We'll leave the car at the lumberyard," he said, "and take our motorboat to Melrose."

"Good!" exclaimed Nan happily. "I love to go places in the *Sunbeam*." The Bobbseys' craft was named for its bright yellow color.

A short time later they were speeding across sparkling blue Lake Metoka. The brisk wind whipped Nan's short hair back from her face. Both twins had high hopes of learning something from the pen they had found at Candy Castle.

Near the far end of the lake Mr. Bobbsey steered into a narrow river. Willow trees lined the banks. Now and then the twins could see a cottage. Finally they came out into another large lake. On the far shore were the buildings of Melrose.

Ten minutes later Mr. Bobbsey docked the boat and the three climbed ashore. Next door was a long, low white building with a red roof. A big sign over the door read: THE JOLLY CRAB.

As Nan glanced at it, she noticed a burly man lounging against the building. His black eyes were fastened on the Bobbseys, but he quickly glanced away.

Mr. Bobbsey said to the twins, "I'll be busy all afternoon. We'll have supper in THE JOLLY CRAB and you can tell me what you found out." He glanced at his watch. "Let's meet here at six."

"Okay," said Bert. "Nan and I'll go to the bank and see what we can find out about that pen. Then we'll go to a movie."

The twins hurried off to a large stone building on the main street. They went up marble steps and entered a big room. At one side were half a dozen men seated at desks behind a mahogany rail. A gray-haired man whose desk sign read *Mr. Knox* looked up at them. "May I help you children?" he said, smiling.

"Yes, thank you. We'd like to ask some questions," Nan replied. She introduced herself and Bert.

Her twin explained their connection with the mystery at Happy Island.

"I understand," Mr. Knox said. "The police were here this morning and showed us the pen that you found at the castle. I can tell you only what I told them. In February of this year the bank had an anniversary. To celebrate it we gave a pen to each customer."

Bert groaned. "I guess there were hundreds of them."

"Did you give them to anyone else?" Nan asked.

"No," said the man, "but some were stolen. At that time the bank was robbed during business hours."

The twins nodded. "We read about it," said Bert.

Mr. Knox went on, "One of the robbers saw a box of the pens and helped himself."

"What did he look like?" Bert asked eagerly.

"I really couldn't say," replied the bank officer. "All three of the robbers were masked. He was quite a small fellow, though."

Bert and Nan exchanged excited looks. "It could have been the little man who stole our cash box at Tiny Town. We think he's connected with the trouble at the castle," said Bert.

Mr. Knox frowned. "You never can tell. The police suspect which gang it was. Their leader is Fancy Jim Jones. He's called that because he wears sporty clothes. His two pals are Ben Gill and Lifty Lemon. Lifty's the one who took the pens. He got this nickname because he can't resist lifting anything that's lying around."

Mr. Knox went on, "With every policeman in the area looking for these men, all the gang wouldn't dare hang around an amusement park picking pockets.

"I think those three men are hiding as far away from here as possible with their loot. By the way, they have not spent one dollar of it yet."

Mr. Knox explained that the serial numbers on the bills were known and police all over the country were watching for the money to turn up.

"It's certainly well hidden—as well as they are!" the bank officer added.

When the twins were outside once more Nan said, "Do you suppose the gang could have buried the stolen money on Happy Island?"

"How could they?" Bert argued. "The police would have found it by now."

Nan shrugged. "Those pens were given out in February. By now anybody could have one, and that's no clue."

Bert agreed gloomily. After lunch and a movie, the twins walked around town, then met their father at THE JOLLY CRAB.

The hostess placed them at a table by an open window. Just outside it was a narrow wooden gallery overlooking the water. A row of motorboats rocked at anchor beneath it.

After consulting the large menus, all three ordered seafood dinners.

"Now tell me what you found out," said Mr. Bobbsey.

As Bert was telling the story, Nan suddenly

put a finger to her lips and motioned the others to listen. A board creaked outside the window.

Quietly Bert and his father moved back their chairs, stood up, and looked over the low sill. Crouched on the gallery was a burly man with black hair.

"Grab him!" Bert shouted.

He and Mr. Bobbsey seized the fellow's shirt. With a gasp the man jerked free, swung under the railing, and dropped out of sight.

The Bobbseys dashed from the restaurant. They were just in time to see the man speed away in a black motorboat.

"He's the one I saw this morning," said Nan. "He was standing right here and probably heard our plans."

"Two eavesdroppers in less than twenty-four hours!" said Mr. Bobbsey grimly.

"This one," Bert told him, "isn't the same fellow who was outside our house last night. That man left small footprints."

"I'm sure," said Nan, "that he's a friend of this one. That's how the big man knew we'd be here today."

Bert looked thoughtful. "They must have been very anxious to learn what we found out about that pen."

Puzzling over the case, the Bobbseys went back into the restaurant. They ate a delicious dinner, then headed for home in their boat.

"Grab him!" Bert exclaimed

By the time they reached Lake Metoka, it was dusk. The lights of the amusement park twinkled in the distance.

As they passed a small wooded island, the twins saw a log house in a clearing. It was dark, but Bert spotted a black motorboat on the beach. He pointed it out to the others.

"That could be the boat the eavesdropper just used and maybe the same one that followed us last night."

"That's right," agreed Mr. Bobbsey, turning on his light. "But there's more than one black motorboat on this lake."

Just then Nan cried, "Oh, look, isn't that beautiful!" She pointed up to a plane pulling a streamer of lighted letters:

COME TO HAPPY ISLAND

"That's Flying Phil!" said Bert. The children waved and shouted.

"I hope Skip found Mop this morning," said Nan. "Wouldn't it be wonderful!"

The next moment Bert seized his father's arm. "Dad! Put into Happy Island! Please!" he shouted over the roar of the motor.

CHAPTER VIII

THE SAND PIRATE

MR. BOBBSEY steered the *Sunbeam* toward the amusement park.

"What's on your mind, Bert?" he asked.

"If Skip hasn't found Mop, he could advertise for the dog with a lighted streamer from his father's plane," said Bert. "Phil could tell us how to make it."

"That's great," Nan said. "And while Phil flies around with the sign, maybe one of us could make an announcement on the loudspeaker. We'll offer a reward to anyone who finds Mop."

Mr. Bobbsey nodded. "Both are excellent ideas."

As soon as they docked, the twins hastened to Flyaway Hill. Skip was standing at one side of the lighted field watching the plane overhead.

"Skip!" Nan called. "Did you find Mop?"

The tall boy turned and shook his head glumly.

"We have a plan!" Bert said breathlessly and explained what the twins wanted to do.

Nan added, "Would it take long to get the letters?"

Skip's eyes were sparkling. "We have everything we need!" he said. "Come on!"

He trotted to a low shed and unlocked it. Inside was a metal locker filled with large square pieces of canvas. Small red light bulbs were sewn onto them in the form of letters of the alphabet.

"These squares are connected on wires like Christmas tree lights," Skip explained. "Electrical power is provided by the plane's generator. There's a switch in the cockpit. When you turn it on, the letters light up. We can make any combination we want to. What shall we say?"

"How about 'Help find the dog Mop,' " Bert suggested. "And our phone number."

"That's good," said the red-haired boy. "Here's an H. Let's get going."

In a few minutes the letters were together. The children had just finished when the plane landed. They ran over to it.

"Dad!" Skip called as the flier started to get out. "Wait a minute, please!"

The boy made his request and Phil said, "That's a good idea! Attach your message."

The twins followed curiously as Skip hurried to the tail of the plane. The sign which had advertised Happy Island was removed and the banner carrying their message was attached to the craft by means of a long towing cable.

"We're all set for takeoff, Dad!" Skip shouted. "Shall I work the light switch?"

"Okay," the pilot said. Then seeing Bert's eager look, he added, "You may come too. Just make sure the safety belt fits around you and Skip."

"I'll run and tell Mr. Flotow to start announcing!" said Nan and dashed off.

The boys climbed into the front cockpit. Skip pulled two helmets and goggles from under the seat and handed one to Bert. After adjusting the seat belt, he signaled his father that they were ready.

"Here we go!" the pilot yelled.

Bert adjusted his goggles as the plane roared down the runway. There was a slight tug as the cable pulled the sign off the ground behind them.

"This is keen!" Bert shouted when the nose of the craft pointed skyward.

The bright lights of the park grew smaller as the flier circled over the lake. Skip turned on the light switch. At once the sign behind them became a glowing ribbon. For more than a quarter of an hour they flew over the lake and amusement park with the message about Mop streaming out behind them.

Then a tiny white light flashed on the panel. "It's Dad's signal that we're going in to drop the sign and land," said Skip.

"Let me do it," Bert asked.

"Okay. Just pull out the release handle to your left."

Moments later they landed.

"That was really great!" said Bert as he jumped to the ground beside the Brewsters.

"Aerobatics are more fun," said Skip. "Dad's going to teach me to do them someday. So far I can only fly."

Bert's eyes grew big. "You know how to fly this plane? You mean it?"

"Sure. Dad taught me."

"He's pretty good," said Phil, "but too young for official lessons or a pilot's license."

"I have a key for the plane, though," said Skip with a grin.

"Put the streamer in the equipment shed," his father told him. "We'll fly it again tomorrow night if you don't find Mop."

The boys put it away, then hurried down the hill toward the Administration Building. Nan was waiting in front for them.

"I made the announcement," she said. "Let's hope somebody answers it."

Early the next morning Freddie hopped out of bed and shouted, "Bang! Bang! Happy Fourth of July!" After that there was no more sleep for anyone. To their disappointment no word came about Mop. Finally Nan suggested that they go swimming at the island.

"We can take a picnic lunch, stay all day, and see the fireworks tonight."

The young twins whooped with excitement. "Oh please, Mommy, let's do it!" Flossie cried.

"All right," said Mrs. Bobbsey with a smile. "I'll take you. How about the rest of you?"

"Oh yes," Bert said.

"You can't leave me out." Mr. Bobbsey grinned.

Half an hour later Skip and the Bobbseys boarded a launch for the park. At the dock the red-haired boy said good-by and went to Flyaway Hill.

Carrying the lunch and their bathing bags, the twins led the way down the dirt road to the sandy beach which curved partway around Castle Hill.

Mr. Bobbsey paid admission and they all entered a long white locker house. A short time later the twins and their parents met on the beach in their swim suits.

"There aren't many people here today," said Nan. "I guess business is still bad on account of Mr. Kruger's disappearance."

Big towels were spread out in front of the rocky hillside. Then Freddie shouted, "Last one in is a tadpole!"

As the children raced for the water, Nan suddenly stopped. She still had her watch on!

Slipping it off, she hid it in a rocky crevice of the hillside. "The watch'll be safe there," she thought. "Nobody can step on it."

After swimming awhile, the twins explored the beach. Rounding a bend, they stopped short in surprise.

"Wow!" Freddie exclaimed.

Flossie's eyes were big as saucers. Before them stood the huge figure of a pirate made of sand!

A sun-tanned man wearing a white sailor hat was working on a giant boot. He had propped a sign against the bluff. It read:

SANDY, THE SAND SCULPTOR.

"Which pirate is it?" Bert asked the man.

"Blackbeard," he replied with a smile. The artist explained that he traveled around the country to resorts and parks making his remarkable figures.

Nan looked puzzled. "How do you keep them from getting damaged?"

Sandy pointed to several tall wooden stakes in the sand and a bundle of plastic rolled up behind them.

"That's a big cover," he said. "At night I throw it over those poles and it makes a tent for the figures. That way they don't get knocked over by accident or melted by rain."

While the others talked to the sculptor, Flossie decided she would like a closer look at the pirate's head. She climbed up the bluff behind the beach. From the top she leaned out to look into the pirate's face.

"Hi, Blackbeard!" she cried, waggling her hand at him. With that she slipped. Yelling, Flossie slid down the bluff straight for the sand figure!

"She'll knock Blackbeard over!" Nan cried.

Instantly Bert flung himself toward Flossie, pushing her to the side inches from the pirate's boots.

"Wow!" said Freddie. "That was close!"

Bert helped Flossie to her feet. Red-faced, the little girl apologized to the sculptor.

"Okay. No harm done," he said kindly.

The twins strolled back to the bathing beach and played in the water some more. At noon they picked up their towels and went to get dressed. Skip met the family in a picnic grove at the foot of Flyaway Hill. They bought milk at a nearby stand.

"Um, this is good," he said, biting into a chicken sandwich Dinah had prepared.

There were also peanut butter and jelly sandwiches and homemade cake for dessert. Afterward the boys gathered up the trash and put it in a red barrel near their table.

"I have to go now," said Skip. "See you tonight at the fireworks."

"She'll knock Blackbeard over!"
Nan cried

"Where are they going to be?" Flossie asked.

"Flyaway Hill," Skip replied.

During the afternoon the twins enjoyed the various rides. They had so much fun that it was not until the middle of the fireworks that Nan suddenly remembered her watch.

"It's still on the beach!" she told her twin.

"You *hope*," said Skip, who had heard her.

"Let's get it," said Bert. "We can be back before the fireworks are over."

Nan explained to her parents, who were standing nearby with the young twins and Mr. Flotow. Then the trio took the chair lift down the hill. As they hurried through the park they could hear the fireworks exploding in the sky behind them. Looking back, they saw showers of colored stars falling over the hill.

"The beach is pretty dark at night," Skip remarked.

"I have my flash," said Bert.

When the three children reached the shore he turned on his light and they plowed through the soft sand. Nan studied the rocky bluff carefully.

"I left the watch about here," she said.

"Wait!" said Bert sharply. "I thought I heard voices!"

The children stood still and listened. The only sound was the water lapping against the shore.

"Nobody's down here," Skip whispered.

"I heard something," Bert insisted softly. "Let's take a look around the bend."

Quietly the three trudged ahead. As they rounded the curve, Bert beamed his flashlight straight ahead. Nan screamed. The huge figure of Blackbeard was toppling toward them!

CHAPTER IX

BERT TO THE RESCUE

"JUMP!" yelled Bert.

As the children leaped backward, the giant sand figure hit the beach and broke apart. The next instant the flashlight was snatched from Bert's hand and went sailing through the air.

"Run!" shouted a hoarse voice.

Bert heard a splash and spotted his light glowing in the shallow water. He sped over, picked it up and flashed the beam around the beach. It was empty! Who had grabbed the light and yelled?

"This is spooky!" said Nan. In a moment Bert's light came to rest on the ruined statue. "Poor Sandy!" she exclaimed. "Why would anyone want to wreck his work?"

"Here's how it was done," said Bert.

He pointed to an old hatchet lying beside the stumps of the pirate's legs. The plastic cover for the statue lay nearby in a heap. Bert took a handkerchief and wrapped the hatchet in it.

"There's nothing more we can do here," said Nan. With a sad look at the wrecked figure, the three children started back along the beach.

"My watch," Nan reminded the boys, "was about here."

They went with her to the rocky bluff and she felt into the crevice. The watch was still there. She slipped it on.

"You're lucky," remarked Skip. Bert said nothing. He had been quiet since leaving the broken pirate statue. But suddenly he spoke up.

"I've been thinking. There seems to be a lot of sand in this mystery. You know what I mean?"

"That's right," said his sister. "Somebody slashed the sandbags in Tiny Town, and now somebody's knocked down a sand figure. Maybe he's looking for something that's hidden in sand."

Skip spoke up. "What could it be, but who do you think is looking?"

"It might be the Jones gang," said Bert, "but I'm just about the only one who thinks so."

"Whoever these guys are, they play pretty rough," said Skip, "and if I were you—"

"Ssh!" said Nan softly. "Listen! I thought I heard a noise."

Bert swept the light around. No one was in

sight. He played the beam on the bushes and trees above the rocky bluff. Not a leaf stirred.

"What kind of a noise was it?" Skip whispered.

"Sort of a beeping," Nan replied.

"It was probably a frog," said Bert. He laughed softly. "We're getting jumpy."

As they walked on down the beach, the children decided to ask Mr. Flotow for permission to search the castle again that night. As they hurried through the park, skyrockets were still bursting in the air, and the music of the band sounded faintly.

The Promenade was nearly deserted. When the children reached the lift, the empty chairs were moving up and down the hill in ghostly procession. Apparently the attendant had gone off.

Nan stepped onto the low platform and a chair stopped automatically. She got in, fastened the belt and a moment later the chair started up. The boys took the one behind her.

Rising through the darkness, they craned their necks to watch the fireworks. A burst of bright-colored balls seemed to be showering down on their heads.

Nan shaded her eyes and looked down. In the red glare she saw a man stoop over the machinery box beside the chair lift. The next moment the Roman candle went out and all was dark. At the same moment the chairs jerked to a halt and swung in midair.

"What happened?" Bert exclaimed.

"Somebody stopped the machinery!" Nan cried. "I saw him!"

Another bursting shell lit up the hillside. Now there was no one below.

Skip groaned. "This is great! Everybody's up watching the fireworks. How are we going to get out of here?"

"If the machinery's really broken we're stuck until they can fix it," said Bert.

He looked over the edge of his chair to the dark treetops below. A little behind the boys stood one of the metal poles which supported the lift cables.

"I think we can reach that post," Bert said. "Are you game to slide down?"

"Sure thing," Skip replied.

After placing the wrapped hatchet on the floor, Bert opened his seat belt and stood up.

"Look out!" yelled Skip, and Nan screamed when the boys' chair began to swing wildly to and fro. Bert grabbed the side to keep from falling out.

"Hey! Hold it! You'll dump us!" exclaimed Skip.

"Oh Bert, be careful!" Nan begged.

Her twin took a deep breath. "Grab my belt," he said to Skip.

Leaning carefully over the back of the chair, Bert found that he was just able to reach the pole.

"Okay," he said. "I have it! Here I go!"

Bert grasped the pole tightly and climbed out of the chair. It rocked hard, but he hung on tightly. When Bert had slid down the pole, Skip followed. A few minutes later Nan spotted them on the ground running toward the foot of the hill.

For a while nothing happened. Then the chair lift started with a jerk and she was borne to the top of the hill. Nan hurried through the crowd to her family and Mr. Flotow. Breathlessly she told what had happened.

The park owner groaned. "What are those devils trying to do? Ruin me? If only I knew what they wanted!"

Nan repeated Bert's theory. Her father looked interested. "What could be hidden in the sand?" he asked.

"I wish I knew," said Mr. Flotow miserably. "I'd give them the whole lake shore, if they'd just leave my park alone."

In a few minutes Bert and Skip came hurrying up. Bert handed Mr. Flotow something wrapped in a newspaper. "This is what the fellow used to jam the chair lift machinery," he said.

The park owner opened the cloth and showed the others a monkey wrench. "You know what this is?" he asked bitterly. "One of the things that was stolen last week! The rascals are using the tools they took to wreck my park!"

Nan told him about the hatchet they had found at the beach that was still in one of the chairs.

"It's mine, I guess," said Mr. Flotow. "A hatchet was missing, too."

Bert said, "Mr. Flotow, those spooks are really jumping tonight. I think this is a good chance to catch them. Would you let us search the castle again?"

The park owner turned to Mr. and Mrs. Bobbsey. "What do you say?"

Mrs. Bobbsey shook her head. "I don't like the idea," she said quietly. "We mustn't forget that Mr. Kruger vanished from that castle."

"But we ought not to pass up a chance to solve the mystery," Bert pleaded.

"And if a lot of us went," Nan put in, "we couldn't all vanish."

"There's something to that," her father agreed.

"The police were here this morning," said Mr. Flotow. "They didn't find anything. Sup-

"Here I go!"

pose I get one of the park guards to go with us to the castle."

"All right," said Mrs. Bobbsey. She turned to Bert and Nan. "You and Skip come home with Mr. Flotow. Dad and I will take Freddie and Flossie back now.

The band started to play "America, The Beautiful." At one side of the field a giant flag made of lights appeared.

"That's the end now," said Mr. Flotow hastily. "I'll go pick up that hatchet in the chair lift. You children meet me at Candy Castle about five minutes after closing time."

When Nan and the boys arrived, the hill was deserted. The floodlights on the castle went out and the ticket taker came from the gatehouse. He locked the castle door and seemed glad to hasten down the slope. He had not seen the children standing to one side.

A few minutes later Mr. Flotow came puffing up with a park guard. "Well, here we go again!" he said, starting toward the gatehouse.

"Wait!" said Bert. "Let's not turn on the lights. If anybody's in there, it'll scare them out."

"Good idea," said Mr. Flotow. "I'll just get a flashlight." Hastily he unlocked the door to the gatehouse, went in and returned with a large light.

He stepped over to the door of the castle and quietly unlocked it. When the heavy portal swung open the children peered into the dark passage. The next moment a wild shriek split the air. Startled, Nan clutched Bert.

"What was that?" Skip whispered.

"I don't know," the guard replied. "It sounded like it came from the hill behind the castle."

The park owner turned to him. "You find out what it was," he said. "I'll go in the castle."

"Me?" said the guard, looking uncomfortable.

"I'll go with you," Skip spoke up.

"Never mind," said the guard quickly. "That's okay." He walked off.

As Bert started for the dark doorway, Mr. Flotow put a hand on his arm. "No," he said quietly. "I don't like the way this is shaping up. You youngsters wait out here and don't come in unless I call you."

"But it's not safe for you to go in alone," Nan protested. "We ought to stay together." The boys chimed in and tried to convince him.

"Thanks, but I'll go myself," the little man said stubbornly. "I'll call if I want you." With that he walked up the narrow passage and disappeared around the corner.

Nan shivered. "Just like Mr. Kruger," she thought.

After five minutes there came a faint, hollow call, "Bert!"

The children looked at one another. "That doesn't sound like Mr. Flotow," Nan whispered.

"We'd better go in, though," her twin said. "Maybe it's the echo in the castle that makes it sound queer."

Skip agreed. "Come on! He might need us!"

With Bert in the lead, they went up the dark passage. He flashed his light around the main room. Nothing strange was there.

Quietly the trio filed up the spiral staircase and into the throne room. It was empty.

Suddenly Nan stiffened. She had heard a footstep on the landing outside the door. The next moment a weird wail came from somewhere above them. The slide was suddenly bathed in green light.

The children froze in terror as a big, billowing, black object came swooping down the slide toward them!

CHAPTER X

A TINY CLUE

"WATCH out!" Bert shouted. He flung up his arm to ward off the black thing. Instantly the green light went out.

Nothing happened.

Bert aimed his light at the slide. It was empty!

"Whatever that was, slid right on down," Skip whispered.

"It should come out into the courtyard," said Nan.

At that moment a faint bang came from somewhere below.

"What was that?" Skip asked.

"I don't know," said Bert quickly, "but let's get down there fast. Maybe we can catch the thing!"

As they turned toward the door, the children heard a muffled thumping. Once again Bert flashed his light around the room, but could see no one.

"The chest by the throne!" Nan exclaimed. "The noise is coming from there!"

Skip took a deep breath. "You stay behind us, Nan," he said, and the three walked quietly toward the big box.

"You lift the lid," whispered Skip to Bert, "and I'll jump on him—or it."

Bert handed his sister the flashlight. Cautiously he lifted the heavy lid as Skip crouched to spring.

"It's Mr. Flotow!" cried Nan. The white-haired man lay in the chest. His hands and feet were bound and a handkerchief tied across his mouth.

The three children untied him and helped the man climb out. Bert closed the chest lid and the park owner sat down on it.

"What happened?" Bert asked.

"Somebody jumped me," Mr. Flotow replied. "I had just come up the stairs and through the door. The next moment—pow!"

"Did you call Bert before that?" asked Skip. The park owner shook his head.

"Well, somebody did," said Nan.

"I think this whole trick was done to scare us off," said Bert, and told about the black "spook" on the slide.

Just then heavy footsteps sounded on the

stairs. In a moment the park guard burst through the door with his flashlight.

"There's nobody on that hill, Mr. Flotow," he said. "I searched and searched."

Quickly Bert told him what had happened. "The mischief-makers probably spotted you men," said Bert, "and figured a wild yell would draw at least one of you away."

"But that black thing you saw—" the man said. He sounded worried.

"It was pretty scary," Bert admitted, "but we know it must have been a trick of some kind."

"I don't know," the guard said hoarsely. "If it went down the slide like you say, it must have come out into the courtyard."

"That's right," said Nan.

"Then why didn't the electric-eye bell go off?" the guard asked. "I'll tell you why! Because the thing wasn't real, that's why!"

In spite of herself, Nan felt a shiver go down her spine. "Was the alarm turned on?" she asked.

Mr. Flotow nodded. "Yes. It goes on automatically at closing time."

Bert started for the door. "Come on!" he said. "Let's see what we can find."

"I'll search the castle again," said Mr. Flotow grimly. He instructed the guard to watch the front door.

Nan and the boys hurried outside and around

to the rear of the building. Bert shone his light into the courtyard and the black mouth of the tunnel. Both were empty.

"Maybe the spook was somebody under a black cloth," said Nan uncertainly, "but I don't see how he could get out without setting off the alarm."

"That thing wasn't heavy enough to be a person," Skip remarked. "It sort of swayed and billowed."

Bert nodded. "It hardly seemed to touch the slide. There must be *some* kind of a clue!" he burst out. "Let's search every inch of this courtyard!"

With Skip and Nan on either side of him, he paced round the small enclosure, moving the light slowly over the white foam rubber under foot. They found no clue.

"I'll try the slide," said Bert. He dropped to his knees and began to crawl up the polished wood, still holding the flashlight. Suddenly a bell rang loudly. Bert jumped, startled, and he heard exclamations from Nan and Skip in the courtyard.

"The alarm," he thought and crept on. The ringing stopped.

Suddenly he spotted a shred of black cloth caught on a tiny splinter. He picked the fragment off.

"A clue!" Bert thought. Then he noted a

crack in the wood. He followed the hairlike line with his light and saw that it went straight across the slide. Bert tried to crawl farther, but the slippery slope became too steep. He slid back out into the courtyard.

"Here's part of the ghost's robe," he said, and showed Nan and Skip the bit of cloth.

"But what *was* the ghost?"

Nan snapped her fingers. "I know! Remember the bang we heard?"

"A balloon!" both boys cried together.

"Of course!" said Nan. "It caught on the same splinter the cloth did and broke!"

"But where did the cloth go?" Skip wanted to know.

"Somebody must have been waiting here to pick up the balloon and the black cover," Bert answered. "There had to be at least three people in on this trick. One yelled in the woods, another was in the turret to send the balloon down and give that scary howl. A third to hold the green light, that came from behind us."

Thinking over the weird trick, the children walked around to the front of the castle. Mr. Flotow was just coming out the front door.

"Empty again!" said the park owner in disgust.

"Nobody came out this way," the guard said. "I kept my eye right on that door all the time. I don't like this!" he added in a shaking voice.

"This castle's dangerous. I'm quitting this job."

Mr. Flotow sighed. "I can't say I blame you. The new watchman did the same thing this morning. Come on," he added gloomily, "I'll take you all home in my boat."

As the powerful craft cut through the water, the two boys and Nan talked quietly about their enemies in the castle.

"After we found the pirate, one of them must have followed us and overheard our plans," said Nan. "Then he jammed the chair lift to give the others time to get the spook ready."

"What worries me," said Skip, "is that they are trying so hard to get rid of you Bobbseys."

Uneasily the children looked back. There was no sign of a pursuing boat. The castle loomed darkly against the starlit sky. *What was its secret?*

The next day was Saturday. "Today's the big race!" exclaimed Freddie when he hurried to breakfast.

Skip showed no excitement. He was still sad because there was no news of Mop. To cheer him up, Mrs. Bobbsey told him that she had invited his father to join the family at luncheon and the race.

"I wonder," said Bert, "what kind of a car Danny and Jack built. They've been bragging about it for weeks, but nobody's seen it."

Bert had just finished speaking when Charlie

"A clue!" Bert thought

Mason came over on his bicycle to the Bobbsey yard. He, with Bert and Freddie, went into the garage and rolled out the long rocket-shaped car while the other children watched.

Skip whistled. "That's cool!" he said. "What makes it run?"

"Compressed air gives it jet power," said Bert. He explained that a local company had supplied each car with a unit of this air. "You have to rig it up yourself to make it work."

As the three boys began to touch up their entry with silver paint, Mrs. Bobbsey called Nan to the telephone. In a few minutes she burst from the house, her face pink with excitement. "It was the dog pound! The lady there, Mrs. Graves, thinks they have Mop!"

Skip's face lighted up, and Bert stopped painting.

Nan went on, "The lady in charge says somebody told her about our sky sign and we can come over right now to see if the dog is Mop."

"We can ride our bikes," said Flossie.

"You can use mine, Skip," said Bert. "I wish I could go with you, but this car has to be ready for the race."

Twenty minutes later Skip and the girls coasted up to a red brick building on a side street. They hurried inside. Mrs. Graves, a stout lady wearing a smock, sat at a desk.

The children introduced themselves and she

took them into a room with wire cages on both sides. At once the place was filled with loud barking. The woman pointed to a big black dog with long stringy hair lying in the corner of a cage.

The children's faces fell. "That's the wrong dog," said Skip.

The woman nodded kindly. "I'm sorry," she said.

Flossie gazed at the sad-looking dog. "What's the matter with him?"

Mrs. Graves smiled. "He's lonesome. All he needs is a good home. If you hear of anybody who wants him, let me know."

Skip and the girls came out of the pound. Nearby was the old man who had been petting Mop just before the dog ran away. He stopped short when he saw the children.

"Hello," he said in his quavery voice. "Did you find your dog?"

"No," Nan answered. "It was the wrong one."

The old man seemed truly disappointed. "Too bad."

"Mop was so cute." Flossie sighed.

"Yes, I remember," said the old man. "How I'd love to see that little dog again!" He walked slowly around the corner.

The children mounted their bikes and ped- aled around the same corner. They were sur- prised to see the old man standing with his back to a wall. He was holding up the lapel of his coat and talking quietly to the flower in his buttonhole!

As the children passed, he looked up, startled. "Just smelling the pretty posy!" he called feebly.

"What's he talking about?" Nan thought. "That flower is not real. It's plastic!"

CHAPTER XI

THE BIG RACE

"THERE'S something fishy about that old man," said Skip. "It looked as if he was talking to the flower in his lapel!"

"Yes," Nan agreed. "And it's funny that we ran into him right here where we came to find Mop."

Skip nodded. "I just remembered something. I saw him the other day when I went to check out that other lead on Mop."

"You think he's following us?" Flossie asked.

"If he is, it seems to be because of Mop," said Nan.

"Perhaps he's a dognapper," Skip suggested. "After all, Mop is a performer. The man might be able to get a lot of money for him."

"I'll bet that's it!" Nan exclaimed.

Flossie's eyes grew round with alarm. "If he finds Mop before we do, he'll steal him!"

"We won't let him!" Freddie declared.

That afternoon the silver rocket car was loaded into the back of the Bobbsey station wagon. When the family arrived at the ball park with Skip, a crowd of spectators was already assembled. A race track had been marked out that circled the field. Charlie was there and helped roll the silver rocket to the starting line.

A few minutes later a long, box-shaped red car was wheeled next to it by Danny and Jack. Both boys wore red shirts and matching caps.

Danny glanced over at Bert and Charlie's sleek-looking car. His face clouded. "Did you make that all yourself?" he asked.

Jack added, "It's against the rules to have any grownups help you."

"We put it together ourselves," Bert said quietly.

"Yeah, I'll bet," Danny smirked. He whispered something to his partner. Jack nodded and grinned.

Meanwhile Freddie and Flossie were walking toward the popcorn stand at the side of the field.

"There's the man with the pipe!" Flossie exclaimed, as they passed the back of the grandstand.

As they watched, the burly fellow lifted the bowl of the pipe to his lips.

"He's talking into his pipe!" Freddie exclaimed.

"He's talking into his pipe!"
Freddie exclaimed

"He certainly does funny things with it," said Flossie.

Puzzled, the children went on to the refreshment stand and bought popcorn. When they walked back toward the starting line, the twins were munching happily. All at once Freddie stopped with a handful of popcorn in midair.

"Look!" he cried. "That's the man with the beeping cane!" He nodded toward a well-dressed man standing near the park fence. The fellow glanced around, then raised the gold head of the stick to his lips.

"He's talking, too!" Flossie exclaimed.

Freddie frowned. "Something awfully funny is going on around here! Let's tell Bert."

But when they reached the starting line, the race was almost ready to begin.

"Freddie, get the helmets," Bert ordered crisply.

His brother hurried to a little suitcase which he had laid on the ground behind the car. He took out two silver-painted helmets and two sets of goggles.

Bert and Charlie put them on. Just then a voice came over the loudspeaker warning the crowd to beware of pickpockets. "There have been a number of complaints already. Watch your purses and wallets."

Bert took the wheel and Charlie climbed in beside him. They hunched forward as the an-

nouncer began the countdown. Then a pistol
shot rang out.

WHOOSH! With a loud hiss of escaping air
the cars started down the track. The silver
rocket shot into the lead. Danny's box came close
behind and veered toward Bert.

"Get over there!" Charlie yelled at Danny.
"You're crowding us!"

Danny grinned, and the red car squeezed the
silver one closer to the spectators. As Bert cast a
quick glance at them, he saw the old man who
had petted Mop standing in the front row. The
next moment Danny swerved closer. Bert jerked
his wheel to avoid a collision and the rocket car
shot straight for the old man.

"Look out!" Bert yelled and the spectators
screamed.

The man leaped nimbly out of the way and
ran off as the boy jammed on the brakes. Bert
stopped inches from the crowd.

Although shaken by the near accident, Bert
was more excited by a discovery he had made.
"Charlie, that fellow's not really old!" he exclaimed. "Did you see him run off?"

But Charlie was looking angrily after the
other cars. "Wait till I get Danny Rugg and
Jack Westley. They made us lose the race!"

Ten minutes later when the results were announced, the silver rocket team felt better. They
had won the prize for the best-designed car.

Danny and Jack had been disqualified for crowding. Bert and Charlie, each carrying a trophy, congratulated the winners, then went home.

Later as the Bobbseys and their guests were drinking iced lemonade on the front porch, Bert told about the man he had nearly hit with his car. "He's not really old," he said. "That's just a disguise. And you know what I think—"

"I'll bet I do!" put in Nan. "You think he's the young man who stole our cash box."

"That's right. Two reasons. Both men are little, and both wear those pink plastic flowers."

"Then he's part of the castle gang!" said Skip.

"But why does he talk to the flower?" Flossie asked. She and Freddie told about seeing him. "And another man talks into his pipe."

"Two-way radios!" Bert exclaimed.

"Of course," said Skip. "The men have tiny walkie-talkies hidden in the flower, the pipe and the top of the cane."

"That beeping sound is probably the signal to listen," Bert added.

Mr. Bobbsey nodded. "I believe you have discovered something," he said. "Probably those three fellows are the pickpockets who were in the crowd this afternoon. The leader keeps in touch with them by radio, and they're never seen together. Pretty clever."

Skip remarked that the little man was probably a dognapper, too.

"I have a strong hunch that he's Lifty Lemon, the bank robber," said Bert.

Nan agreed. "Mr. Knox at the bank said that Lifty is small."

"I think the one with the cane is Fancy Jim Jones," Bert went on. "And the other fellow is the one in the workman's clothes, Ben Gill."

"He's real big," said Freddie, "and has mean black eyes."

"Sounds like the eavesdropper at THE JOLLY CRAB," Nan remarked.

"It must be the Jones gang," Bert decided.

"Hold on now," said Mr. Bobbsey. "I go along with the radio theory for the pickpockets, Bert, but those bank robbers wouldn't risk showing themselves just to pick a few pockets or steal a dog."

"I'm sure those are only sidelines," Bert insisted. "Their real game has something to do with the castle."

The next morning, after a delicious Sunday breakfast of sausages and pancakes topped with fresh blueberries, the Bobbsey family went to church. The lovely, warm day passed without any mysterious interruptions.

Monday morning Nan awoke early. She was very hungry and decided to go downstairs for something to eat. As she passed the hall telephone, it began to ring. At once she picked it up.

"Hello."

A boy's voice said, "Mop is in Cliffside on Drake Street." Then the caller hung up.

"Who was it?" asked Mrs. Bobbsey, coming down the stairs. "By the time I picked up the extension, the person was gone."

Just then Flossie padded down the stairs. She had missed her sister. Nan told her mother and Flossie about the call.

"It may have been a joke," Mrs. Bobbsey said.

"But shouldn't we go and see anyway?" Flossie suggested. "Please, Mommy, let Nan and me go."

Nan was eager too. "We'll be all right. Floss and I can go over and back on the bus. If this is a false alarm, Skip won't have to be disappointed again." Nan's eyes sparkled. "But if we do find Mop, think how happy everybody will be!"

"All right," said Mrs. Bobbsey. "You get dressed and I'll fix some breakfast for you."

The girls caught a bus which went across town to Cliffside. After what seemed like a long ride, they got off at Drake Street which was at the top of a cliff. They looked down the slope at dozens of houses. The street zigzagged downward to a drop-off. A single metal railing ran across, serving as a fence. Lake Metoka sparkled far below.

"It's kind of early to ring doorbells," said Nan. "I see a little girl down there. Let's ask her."

The child, who was about five years old, was seated on her front stoop. She had dark brown pigtails and bangs. Beside her was a doll carriage and a small suitcase.

"Hello," Flossie called, skipping ahead. "What's your name?"

"Amy Wood," she replied. "What's yours?"

Flossie told her. "May we see your baby?" she asked, and peered into the carriage. *"Mop!"* she cried.

Tucked under the covers, and wearing a white bonnet, was the little black dog. At Flossie's voice he struggled out of the cover and stood on his hind legs. He was wearing a long nightgown. Nan gave a cry of delight and reached for the dog.

"No! No!" Amy exclaimed. "He's mine!" As she grabbed for Mop, the little girl stumbled and fell against the carriage. It rolled out of the yard and into the street. Down the road it went, faster and faster!

"Catch it!" Flossie shrieked as Nan dashed ahead.

"Jump, Mop!" cried Nan. "Jump!"

"He can't! He's tangled in the nightgown!" Amy screamed.

The carriage hit a stone wall near the end of the road. It swerved around, then rolled swiftly downhill toward the drop-off!

CHAPTER XII

DOGNAPPERS!

SWIFTLY Nan cut through two yards to the street below. The rolling doll carriage was almost at the edge of the drop-off! She could hear the shrill barking of the dog trapped inside.

"Catch him!" Flossie screamed.

Nan sprinted across the street. Leaping up, she caught the handle of the buggy. It tipped sideways and the dog flew out!

"Oh, Mop! You're safe!" cried Flossie, running up.

Her sister picked up the little black dog. He barked wildly, but as she petted him, he quieted down. "It's all right now," she said soothingly. She smoothed the nightgown he was wearing and straightened his cap. "Poor Mop! You've had such a scare!"

Just then Amy caught up to them. "Give him to me!" she cried. "He's mine!" She reached out and tried to take the dog.

"No, dear," said Nan, holding Mop firmly. "He belongs to a friend of ours, Skip Brewster."

"He's mine!" the little girl insisted, red-faced. "I found him in our yard yesterday morning and my mommy said I could keep him."

"But the boy who owns him wants him back," said Flossie. "Didn't you hear the 'nouncement on TV or see it in the newspaper?"

The little girl shook her head and Nan explained who Mop was and how he had come to be lost.

The child's lips quivered. "You mean I have to give him back?"

Big tears rolled down Amy's cheeks. "But he's so cute," she sobbed, "and I took such good care of him! He was all tired and dirty when he came. I fed him some nice warm milk and dog food, and gave him a bath in my dolly tub. And I let him have my best doll clothes and that little suitcase to keep 'em in. But I didn't let him wear the little necklace." She burst into louder sobs.

"There, there," said Nan, patting the child's shoulder. She took Amy's hand and they started up the street with Flossie dragging the carriage.

Nan had an idea. "Don't cry, Amy," she said. "We'll get you another dog in place of Mop."

Amy caught her breath. "You will? Where is he?"

"In the pound. He's a little bigger than Mop, but he's very lonesome and wants a home."

"When can I have him?" Amy asked.

"I don't know exactly," said Nan, "but soon." The dog in her arms began to squirm. "Hold still, Mop," she said. "You're going home now and—"

Nan broke off with a gasp. The "old" man was coming out of a yard up the street.

"The dognapper!" she exclaimed and turned her back to him.

Flossie's eyes grew wide with fright. "What'll we do?"

"Pretend Mop's a doll," said Nan. She snatched the blanket from the carriage and wrapped it around the dog, so that none of him showed.

Amy started to ask a question and Flossie said, "Shh! He's a bad man."

As Nan turned around, the disguised man was walking feebly toward them. He seemed very surprised to see them.

"Well, hello!" he quavered. "What are you doing way up here?"

"Taking a walk with our friend," said Nan politely, but her heart was thumping. She held Mop tightly and felt his little body twitch.

"I see your dolly is out for an airing, too," he said, looking hard at the bundle in Nan's arms.

"It's a nice day for a walk," said Flossie.

"But we'd better be getting back," added Nan quickly. She smiled cheerfully. "Good-by."

"Pretend the dog's a doll!"
Nan said

The sisters walked on with Amy trotting beside them. Puzzled, she looked back at the man.

"He's watching you," she said.

"Don't look back," Nan muttered, "and don't walk too fast."

The girls forced themselves to stroll casually.

"I think we'd better go into Amy's house and call up Daddy to come and get us," said Flossie.

Nan nodded. "I hope your mother doesn't mind, Amy," she said.

"Course not," said the child. She glanced back quickly. "He's coming this way now."

Nan clutched Mop tighter and walked a little faster. The dog wriggled hard. "Don't do that!" said Nan. "Be quiet!" She stopped squeezing the bundle so tightly.

Suddenly Flossie gasped. "There's the pipe man!" she exclaimed. Nan's heart sank. Coming around the next corner was the burly man who had eavesdropped outside THE JOLLY CRAB!

"Is he bad, too?" whispered Amy loudly.

"Shh!" said Nan, nodding. "I don't think they'll hurt you, though. They're after Mop."

As the man strolled toward them, Flossie said, "We'll have to go past him to get to Amy's."

"Act natural," Nan warned.

The next moment Mop barked loudly!

"It's the dog!" shouted the "old" man. "Get him!"

"Run!" cried Nan. She grabbed Flossie's

hand and dashed through the nearest yard.

"Hurry!" Amy yelled.

Looking back, Flossie saw the little man running swiftly ahead of the burly one. The girls went straight up the steep slope, cutting through yards and across streets. The men kept drawing closer.

"Let's go in a house!" cried Flossie.

"Can't stop!" said Nan. She knew the men would catch up and snatch the dog before anyone could answer the door.

Panting, they had almost reached the cliff-top road when they saw a bus coming.

"Faster!" cried Nan. "We'll catch it."

"I can't—go—any faster," Flossie gasped. Her fat little legs ached and her face was red. But Nan dragged her along. When they came to the top, the bus passed.

"Wait!" Nan yelled. She let go her sister's hand and ran after it, waving wildly.

A block ahead, the bus halted at a stop. A woman got on. Then it started slowly forward.

"Stop! Wait!" the sisters and Amy cried as they ran down the street after it.

The bus stopped. Moments later the frightened girls climbed aboard, red-faced and panting. Amy called good-by and said not to forget the dog they promised her.

"What's your hurry?" the young driver asked with a smile. "Somebody after you?"

"Some bad men were chasing us," said Flossie.

The driver grinned. "Yeah?" He glanced into the rear-view mirror. "I don't see anybody."

The girls looked out the back window. The road was empty.

"I guess they gave up," said Nan.

"Who were they?" asked the young man with a wink. "Three tall guys with purple hair?"

"It's true," said Nan. "We're not joking."

The driver chuckled. "Okay. Have it your way."

Carefully Nan handed the blanket-wrapped dog to Flossie and fished the fare from her pocket. As the two settled themselves on a front seat, they gave a big sigh.

Flossie lifted the edge of the blanket and peeped in at the tiny dog. His black face was framed by the white bonnet and his little pink tongue hung out.

"You're safe now, Mop," Flossie cooed. "Soon you'll be home!" She gave a bounce of excitement. "Won't Skip be surprised?"

"I guess everybody will be," said Nan, smiling.

Flossie rubbed the dog's nose with her finger and he wiggled.

"Cover him up, Floss," said Nan uneasily. "We don't want him to get frisky. I don't think we're supposed to have a dog on the bus."

"All right," her sister said. "But he's so darling." She pretended to kiss his nose, then put the blanket carefully over his face again.

"I wonder how those men knew where we were," said Nan.

Suddenly the driver gave a hoarse shout and the bus swerved sharply. Some of the passengers cried out and Mop barked sharply.

"Shh!" said Flossie.

"Watch where you're going!" shouted the driver angrily as a black car shot ahead of him.

As it roared off, Nan glimpsed the men in it. "The dognappers!" she said to Flossie.

"I wonder why they're in such a hurry," said Flossie.

"I don't know," said Nan, "but there was a black car parked across the street from our house this morning. I'll bet they were spying on us."

The next moment she caught the driver's eye in his mirror.

"Come here a minute," he said to her over his shoulder. Nan walked up and held onto the rail beside his seat.

"Funny thing," he said. "When that car nearly sideswiped us, I thought I heard a dog bark."

Nan flushed. "You did," she admitted.

"You know better than to bring a dog on the bus," he said. "I ought to make you get off."

"Oh, no! Please!" Nan begged. "We couldn't help it. Somebody was chasing us."

"Sure, sure, I heard that before," he said. "Rules are rules, you know—sorry."

"Oh, please," exclaimed Nan, "we're miles from home. And it's true about being chased."

Seeing Nan's worried face, Flossie came over. She listened anxiously as her sister told the driver about finding Mop. "Those men who nearly ran into the bus are the ones who were chasing us," Nan added.

The driver looked surprised. "What do you know! And this is that trick dog I heard about on TV!"

"Mop'll be good," Flossie promised. "You won't even know he's on the bus."

The driver glanced at the girls' worried faces. "Okay, you win," he said.

"Oh, thank you," the sisters chorused.

They returned to their seats. Once more the girls sighed in relief.

"I can hardly wait to get home," said Flossie.

The sisters talked happily of how they would announce the good news. They were so thrilled about rescuing Mop that they paid no attention when the bus pulled up to the next stop.

The dognapper disguised as an old man swung aboard. "I'll take that dog!" he snapped.

Before the startled girls could protect the dog he snatched Mop and leaped off the bus!

CHAPTER XIII

TALKING CANE

"STOP!" Nan cried.

She and Flossie jumped off the bus and ran after the thief. The little man dashed around the corner to a black car. He tossed the blanket-wrapped dog through the open door. Then he swung in and the automobile sped off.

"Oh!" cried Flossie, and burst into tears. "We lost Mop again," she added as the bus driver came running up.

"Did you get the license number?" he asked.

Nan shook her head. "It was all covered with dust."

"Yes, I know," the driver said. "I tried to see it after they nearly rammed the bus. Come on," he added kindly. "I go right past the police station. I'll drop you off. Maybe they can help."

Fifteen minutes later the girls were seated in the office of their friend, Chief Smith. He listened quietly as Nan reported the whole story. The officer said he would start a search at once for Mop.

"We're sure now that the little man isn't really old," she said. She explained Bert's theory about the three thieves carrying walkie-talkies.

"Bert and I think those men are the Jones gang," Nan added.

"That's impossible," the chief said. "I was talking to the Melrose Police this morning, and they just had a call from Florida. A man who wouldn't give his name said the gang had been seen there only an hour ago.

"By the way," the chief said, taking a small brown envelope from his desk drawer, "here are the boys' handkerchiefs. Tell them thanks for being so careful about fingerprints on the tools and pen."

"Did you find any?" Nan asked.

"Plenty. But they were all smudged."

"That's too bad," said Nan. "Is there any news about Mr. Kruger?"

The chief frowned. "Not a trace of him. Police all over the country have his description, but so far we've had no good leads. We'll keep trying, though."

The chief stood up, shook hands with the girls and wished them luck as they left. With heavy hearts they went home and turned up their front walk.

Suddenly Nan tripped. A snicker sounded.

"Enjoy your trip?" asked a voice. Danny stepped from behind a bush by the house. Jack followed, grinning. They walked over and Jack picked up a black thread from the sidewalk.

"See how we fixed it?" he said, pointing to two sticks in the ground on either side of the walk. "We just stretched the thread across."

Nan tightened her lips and said nothing.

Danny laughed. "We fixed up your other trip, too—the one to Cliffside." Then he added, "We heard some little kid at the car race telling another girl how she had found a stray dog. She said she lived on Drake Street in Cliffside."

Jack rocked on his heels. "We hid across the street and saw you come out this morning. Boy, were you in a hurry!"

"You didn't see an old man by any chance, did you?" Nan asked calmly.

"How did you know?" said Danny, surprised.

"He saw us laughing after you left," said Jack, "and wanted to know what the joke was. So we told him."

The girls exchanged looks.

"He got into a black car and drove off with some other fellow," said Danny. He grinned. "Boy, are you stupid! You might have known it was a phony tip."

"For your information," Nan said coldly, "you did us a favor. We found the dog."

The boys were amazed. Then Danny's eyes narrowed and he said, "Where is he?"

"Those men stole him from us," Nan replied. In spite of herself, tears filled her eyes. The bullies stared, too surprised to say anything.

"I think you're the meanest boy in the whole wide world, Danny Rugg!" Flossie burst out. She and Nan hurried into the house.

Mrs. Bobbsey listened sympathetically to her daughters' story. "We expected to be back in time to go to Happy Island," Nan finished, "but it took so long."

"Your brothers left a little while ago with Skip," said her mother. "You can meet them this afternoon, and stay there for the evening."

Flossie watched Dinah preparing lunch. Suddenly the little girl said, "I just thought of something terrible! What if those dognappers try to steal Snap and Waggo? They might even be catnappers and take Snoop, too!"

"Don't you worry about that, honey," said Dinah. She was cutting a large butterscotch cake while her husband watched. "If they come around here, I'll make 'em sorry!"

Sam chuckled. "And they'd better look out for Dinah. She can swing a mean rolling pin!"

Flossie and Nan giggled as they pictured Dinah chasing the thieves with a rolling pin.

After lunch the sisters took a launch to Happy Island and found the boys beside the equipment shed at Flyaway Hill. They looked up as the girls walked over.

"Where were you?" asked Bert. "Mother wouldn't tell us."

Nan grinned. "Just doing a little detective work." She did not want to alarm Skip by telling him the truth.

Bert guessed this and asked, "You girls want to help us? We're testing the light bulbs on all Phil's letters."

"I'd rather play on the beach," said Flossie.

"Me too," Freddie added.

"Go ahead," said Bert, "but meet us back here in an hour." The young twins hurried off.

"Let's go barefoot," Flossie suggested.

Carrying their socks and shoes, they trudged along, digging their toes into the hot sand. They passed a handful of bathers, but otherwise the beach was empty. They sat down near several large rocks and began to build a sand castle.

Suddenly a man's voice said, "We're back, boss. It's not on him." Startled, the children looked around. Nobody was in sight!

"The Bobbsey twins must have it," the voice said plainly. "We'd better get those kids fast!"

The children jumped up and gazed around again. No one! Then Freddie spotted the big gold-headed cane leaning against the rock bluff.

"Why don't you answer, boss?" asked the voice.

It was the cane talking!

The next moment the twins saw the owner, dressed in a gray suit, come from behind a large rock. His back was turned to them and he was dragging a beach chair.

Quietly the children picked up their shoes and fled. At the end of the beach, they put them on again and raced through the park to Flyaway Hill. They found the older children just finishing the light job.

Breathlessly, the twins poured out their story. The listeners looked puzzled.

"What was the voice talking about?" asked Bert. "What is it we're supposed to have?"

"And who is the 'him' who didn't have it on?" Nan added. No one could guess.

"You'd better watch out," declared Skip. "They're after you!"

"Let's report the man on the beach to Mr. Flotow," said Nan. "He can send some park guards to pick him up."

Skip glanced at the sky where the red plane was circling. "I hate to miss the fun. I'll leave a note to tell Dad where I'm going," he said.

After locking the letters in the shed, he scribbled a sentence on a scrap of paper and tacked it on the door. Then the five hurried toward the Administration Building. Nan spotted the man with the cane.

"Let's follow him," said Bert. Minutes later

It was the cane talking!

the man reached Castle Hill and boarded the moving sidewalk.

"We'll have to stick with him," Bert said. "Freddie, you get Mr. Flotow."

"Okay," said his brother and dashed off.

The others raced up the wooded slope a little distance from the moving walk. From behind the trees they watched the man with the cane reach the top, buy a ticket and enter the castle. A moment later the workman with the pipe arrived and did the same.

"It looks as if they're having a meeting," Skip remarked.

"Maybe they'll pull their vanishing trick," said Bert. "If we go in we might catch them at it."

"But suppose they escape by the slide," said Nan. "Somebody ought to watch at the courtyard."

"Okay," said Bert. "I'll cover the exit. Nan, you go inside with Skip. Flossie, wait here for Mr. Flotow and tell him where we are."

As Bert hurried away, Skip bought two tickets and entered the castle with Nan. Except for a few children, the big place was deserted. Nan and Skip looked carefully, even in the chest beside the throne, but found no trace of the men.

"Maybe they went out by the slide," said Skip.

When he and Nan reached the turret, it was

empty except for the young attendant who handed them burlap sacks to sit on.

"Did two men go down here in the past few minutes?" asked Nan.

"No," the boy replied. "Just a few kids. Business is terrible."

Nan sat down at the top of the slide. With a squeal she started down. After a breathtaking ride she landed in the soft courtyard. Skip was behind her.

"Did you see the men?" Bert asked as Nan and Skip came through the courtyard gate.

"No," his sister replied.

"They haven't come out this way either," said Bert.

Just then Flossie raced up with Freddie, Mr. Flotow and a guard.

"Did either of the men go out the front?" Nan asked her quickly.

"No. I watched the whole time."

Quietly Bert reported what had happened. As he finished, Nan glanced down the hill. Between the trees she could see a patch of the beach. Something yellow glinted in the sun. She looked hard.

"That's impossible!" she exclaimed.

"What are you talking about?" asked Bert.

Nan pointed to the beach. There stood the man with the cane!

CHAPTER XIV

THE DARK COVE

"HOW did that man get there?" Bert asked. He stared down the hill at the beach.

"Who?" asked the young twins together.

"I don't see anybody," said Mr. Flotow. He and the guard peered through the trees where Nan had been pointing.

"I did," Skip spoke up excitedly. "It was the man with the cane. He's gone now."

"A little while ago he went into the castle," Nan said. "We couldn't find him inside and he didn't come out by the slide or the front door."

"And yet, there he is—way down on the shore!" Skip exclaimed.

"There must be a secret passage from the castle to the beach," Bert said firmly.

Mr. Flotow shook his head. "Bert, I've told you before, I know every exit in the castle. There's no secret way out."

"But there may be one through the old cellar the castle is built over," Bert said.

"It wouldn't matter," Mr. Flotow argued, "because there's absolutely no way to get from the castle to the cellar."

"We've searched every inch of that fun house over and over," said the guard. He looked hard at Nan. "Are you sure that was the man with the cane you saw on the beach just now?"

"Yes," she replied.

The guard appeared doubtful. "I'll take a look around," he said, and started down the hill.

Mr. Flotow sighed. "Poor Kruger. Gone without a trace! Spooks in the castle! Tiny Town wrecked! Pickpockets ruining my business! Where will it all end?"

"You mustn't give up, Mr. Flotow," Nan said. "We've found out a lot." She told about the gang of pickpockets and how the old man was really a young one in disguise.

Mr. Flotow smiled. "Yes, you have uncovered a lot." He patted Bert's shoulder and walked off.

Nan suggested that they hurry to the beach and see if they could find the man with the cane. The others agreed. They went quickly down the wooded hill behind the castle. A few minutes later they came out of the trees atop the little bluff where Flossie had fallen. The sand sculptor was below, rolling up his large plastic sheet. Nearby lay the ruins of the pirate.

"Hi, Sandy!" called Bert as the children scrambled down. "What are you doing?"

"Packing up," the man replied grimly. He dropped the roll of plastic into a green wooden chest which stood open on the beach.

"We're doing our best to solve the mystery of your Blackbeard," said Bert. "Right now we're looking for a well-dressed man with gray hair who carries a gold-headed cane. Did you see him around here?"

Sandy looked up at them. "As a matter of fact, I did. He came out of the cove." Sandy pointed behind him. "I think he was surprised to see me."

"You mean people don't usually go in there?" Bert asked.

Sandy shook his head and dropped a few tools into the box. "No. It's just a tangle of roots and bushes and rocks. I can't figure out why anybody'd want to walk there. Especially a fellow dressed up the way he was. Besides—" Sandy bit his lip as if he had decided to say no more. Then he started closing the green chest.

"Besides what?" Bert asked. "Is there something else about the cove?"

Sandy hesitated a few moments, then said, "I kind of hate to mention this, because it sounds so silly, but there's something funny about that place."

"What do you mean?" Skip asked eagerly.

"Well, I hear noises there and a voice," the man said, "but when I go to investigate nobody's there."

"You mean a voice in the woods?" Nan persisted.

"No, not exactly. This sounds more as if it was coming from down *inside* the earth," the sculptor said.

The children glanced at one another in excitement. "What kind of a voice is it?" Nan asked.

"Very far away," said Sandy. "And it calls 'Help!'" The sculptor frowned. "Sometimes I'm not even sure I heard it."

"Is that all you can tell us about it?" Bert asked.

"Well, just a little while ago I heard a weird howl—sort of far off, like the voice."

"Is that why you're leaving?" Freddie asked.

"That's part of it," Sandy admitted, "but I don't see any sense in making sand sculptures just to have somebody knock 'em down. There are plenty of other places I can work."

"I wish you would stay a little longer," said Nan. "Maybe the mystery will be solved soon."

"I'll be in Lakeport for a couple of days with friends," Sandy replied.

The children said good-by to the sculptor, wished him luck and walked on down the beach. Where it curved into the cove, they had to go single file, for it narrowed to only a path of sand.

Heavy brush grew almost to the water's edge and up to the top of the bluff.

Bert stopped and looked at the hill. Against the blue sky he could see the peppermint top of the Candy Castle turret.

"This cove is right behind the castle," he remarked.

The children followed the deep curve as far as they could. They were stopped by heavy brush growing right out over the water.

"We'll never get through that," Nan remarked.

Her twin looked puzzled. "I thought there might be a secret entrance into the bluff somewhere. If there were, the bushes in front of it would probably be broken. But all of this looks okay."

"Where's Flossie?" asked Freddie.

His twin was gone!

"Flossie!" Nan called.

"Here I am!" came a giggly voice. Flossie's blond head poked through the brush. "It's not so thick as it looks here," she explained. "I slipped through, and guess what? There's a hollow place back here. You can walk behind this big bunch of brush."

Suddenly, there was a crackling of twigs on the bluff. The others glanced up. A big boulder was tearing down through the bushes. It plunged straight toward Flossie!

"Watch out!" cried Bert.

Instantly Skip yanked her aside. The next moment the rock crashed into the brush right where she had been standing.

Nan put her arm around Flossie, who was shaking with fright. Bert and Skip were already plunging through the brush toward the bluff. They scrambled up the steep slope. At the top they found a pocket of fresh earth where the rock had been resting.

"It was set in pretty deep," Bert said, inspecting the hole carefully. "I think it would have had to be pushed."

Skip agreed. Quietly as they could, the boys made their way along the top of the bluff, but saw no one. They returned to the cove.

"We'd better get out of here," Bert said, hurrying the young twins in front of him.

"About that hollow place behind the bushes, Floss," said Nan. "Does it go anywhere?"

"I don't know."

"I think we ought to come back and explore the cove later," said Bert.

Skip agreed. "If the spooks are hanging around here, we'll give them time to clear out."

This suited Flossie, and all the children returned to the park, where Flossie and Freddie went to Kiddieland to play on swings and slides.

As the older children walked through the park, Skip glanced up and saw his father's plane

"Watch out!" cried Bert

come in for a landing on the hill. "I'll go up and ask Dad if he wants me to help him," he said. "See you later."

"Okay," Bert replied, "we'll let you know before we tackle the cove."

As Skip walked off, Nan and Bert heard their names called over the loudspeaker. "Report at once to Mr. Flotow, please," the announcer said.

Bert and Nan looked at each other in surprise. "I wonder why," said Nan.

In the park owner's office they found a plump girl about their own age. Her face was flushed with excitement.

"This young lady has a lead on Mop," said Mr. Flotow.

"Yes," she spoke up eagerly. "I just heard a girl at an ice cream stand talking about a boy with a little black dog that did tricks. He's over in the picnic ground now."

"Thanks a lot," said Bert. "We'll go there right away."

Excited, the twins hurried to the grove at the foot of Flyaway Hill. A group of people was watching something on the ground. The twins could not see what it was. When they ran over, they heard exclamations of, "Isn't it cute!"

Excited, the Bobbseys wormed their way to the front. A boy stood there beside a tiny black dog which turned round and round on its hind legs.

"Oh, it's a toy!" Nan exclaimed in disappointment. The dog flopped over on its side, whirring.

As the twins left the picnic area, Bert remarked that Skip must have heard the announcement. "He'll be wondering if it was about Mop. We'd better go tell him."

They found the boy and his father at the equipment shed. The flier looked glum. "If business doesn't get any better," he said, "Skip and I'll have to pack up and go."

"Oh, that would be a shame," said Nan. Then, reluctantly, she told about the dognappers. Skip was shocked and downcast.

At nine o'clock that night the two boys and Phil took off again with the sign. Meanwhile, Mr. Flotow announced on the loudspeaker that the dog had been stolen. He described the three suspected men and said that the young curly-haired thief might be disguised as an old man.

When Freddie and the girls came out of the Administration Building, two teenage boys ran up to them. One said they had just seen a small curly-haired man running toward the beach.

Nan thanked them, and they walked on. "Flossie," she said, "you stay here and tell Bert and Skip we've gone to the beach. Maybe Freddie and I can find out where the man's headed."

Nan and her little brother hurried to the shore. Starlight showed that the beach was empty as far as they could see. Nan ran ahead and around the curve, past the stumps of the sand pirate's legs. Freddie tramped behind, unable to keep up.

At the edge of the cove Nan stopped short. It was a dark pocket of water ending in the pitch blackness of the shrubs. Had the man gone in here?

Suddenly from deep in the cove she heard a weird wail!

CHAPTER XV

TIN BOX

A SHIVER went up Nan's spine. She stood still, looking into the dark cove and waited for the eerie howl to come again. There was only silence.

As the wind rose and rustled the brush, Nan heard a faint voice crying, "Help!"

"Who's there?" she called. No one answered.

Freddie came panting up behind her. "What was that awful noise?" he whispered.

"Shh!" said his sister. "I think—" Nan stopped short. Out of the darkness of the cove came the roar of a motorboat. Moments later a black craft passed through into the lake.

Freddie gasped. "Nobody's in the boat!"

At first it seemed as if the boat must be steered by ghostly hands. But as it drew farther from shore three figures suddenly sat up in it.

"The boat must have been hidden in the brush

somewhere," said Nan. "Let's go tell the others quick!"

She and Freddie ran back along the beach. When they rounded the curve, they saw the other twins running toward them with Skip.

"Where did the curly-haired fellow go?" Bert asked as the two groups met.

"Into the cove, I'm pretty sure," Nan replied. Quickly she told what she had heard and about the motorboat.

"Did you see which way it went?" Bert asked eagerly.

Nan shook her head. "It disappeared into the darkness."

"It had no lights," said Freddie, "just like last time."

"What about that voice calling for help?" Skip asked.

Nan hesitated. "I think I heard it," she had to admit. "But I know there was a spooky wail."

"Did you hear the call for help, Freddie?" his brother asked.

"No, but I wasn't there yet," Freddie said.

"I'd like to investigate that cove right now," said Bert, "but we ought to have more than one flashlight."

"There are some up at our equipment shack," Skip said, "Let's get those."

When the children reached Flyaway Hill,

they found Phil locking the shed. Quickly Skip told what had happened at the cove and asked to borrow several flashlights.

"Not so fast," said the pilot. "You leave that cove to the police."

"But Dad—" Skip began.

"Sorry, son," said Phil kindly but firmly. "The answer is no. It's too risky." He glanced at his watch. "There hasn't been anybody up here for the past hour and it looks like rain," he said. "We may as well head for home."

"We'll go with you then," said Bert. He was anxious to talk to his father about the cove and another idea he had.

But when the children reached home, Mr. Bobbsey had already gone to bed. It was not until breakfast that he learned what had happened the night before.

"Dad, the police ought to investigate that cove," Bert said eagerly. "I feel sure they'd find a secret passageway to the castle."

"And I believe," Nan added, "that Mr. Kruger is a prisoner back in the cove somewhere. That would explain the cries for help that Sandy and I heard."

"Another thing," Bert went on, "the boat in the cove last night was black—like the one we saw on the beach of the little island. The police should check there, too. Maybe it's the gang's hideout."

His father looked thoughtful. "You have some good points," he said. "I'll call Chief Smith right away."

Five minutes later Mr. Bobbsey returned to the table. "The chief doesn't buy the idea of the secret passage or of Mr. Kruger's being hidden in it."

"Why not?" Nan asked.

"Because no one has been able to find any opening to a passage in the castle. However, the chief thinks the little island is worth investigating. You older twins will go along to show the police which one it is."

Half an hour later Bert and Nan were speeding across Lake Metoka in the police launch. Their friend, Officer Lane, was at the wheel. Three policemen, Brown, Denver, and Carson, were with him. The twins knew them all.

The sky was gray and a crisp wind made tiny white caps on the dark water. Officer Lane squinted up at the clouds. "I hope we make the island before the storm hits."

"There's the place," said Bert, pointing ahead.

The launch circled the heavily wooded shores, but the searchers saw no boat.

"It may be hidden," said Officer Brown.

As the police launch landed at the beach, Officer Lane cautioned everyone to be quiet. Straight ahead was a two-story log house.

Quietly they went up to it. Brown and Denver went around to the back. Nan and Bert followed the other officers inside. They found no one, but the rooms showed that people had been living in the place.

Officer Lane checked under the beds and looked in the closets. "Nobody here now," he said.

"Maybe the men saw us coming," Bert suggested, "and they're hiding in the woods."

"That's possible," said Lane. "We'll scout around. You and Nan stay on the porch. If these fellows are in the woods they might try to sneak back to the house. In that case, you yell."

As the four men set off, the twins seated themselves on the front steps. They waited without talking.

The wind blew harder and they could hear the waves slapping against the shore. Thunder rumbled in the distance. Suddenly a scuffling noise sounded on the roof. Both children stiffened.

"Maybe a squirrel," Bert said softly.

The next moment there was a louder *thump!* Then a pair of legs appeared over the edge of the porch roof.

"Help! Police!" screamed Nan, while Bert tackled the fellow and yanked him down.

He hit the ground with a yell and a tin box bounced from his hand. He was the short, curly-haired thief! Thrusting Bert away, he jumped up and dashed into the woods.

The boy tore after him, but lost the man in the heavy bushes along the shore. In a moment Bert heard the roar of a motor and saw the black craft burst from the brush and speed away with the three men in it. Minutes later the police launch was speeding across the lake in pursuit.

Suddenly lightning flashed and the storm broke. The rain hit the windshield with blinding force. Drenched, the children and officers sped on, but lost sight of the fleeing boat.

In a short time the rain ceased. But the men and their boat were gone.

"There's no telling where they went ashore," said Lane. "We may as well head for Lakeport."

As they sped back, Nan handed Officer Brown the tin box she had picked up after the thief dropped it. The policeman pried open the lock. Inside were wallets, watches and a brown cloth bag filled with money. On the sack was a tag with the words, "Tiny Town."

"This is the pickpocket's loot all right," said Brown. "We'll return it to the owners as soon as possible."

"There must have been an attic in that house with a trap door leading to it," Bert said. "The fellow was probably hiding there and didn't know we were on the porch."

"I guess the gang saw us coming," said Nan.

"Help! Police!" screamed Nan

"Two of them headed for the hidden motorboat while the other one went to the attic to get the loot."

Officer Denver nodded. "That's probably the way it was. He got trapped there and decided to make a run for it. We'll go back later and check over that house."

Officer Lane thanked the twins for the lead they had provided. Then he grinned at Nan, whose hair was straight and dripping. "We'd better get you home so you can dry off."

That afternoon the four twins worked at Tiny Town. They had permission to stay for supper and go home with Mr. Flotow. An hour before closing time, they met Skip.

"Let's take a look around Candy Castle," said Bert. "Maybe we'll spot one of the men."

The children hurried to the hill and walked around the strange building. Suddenly Nan exclaimed, "Look down there!"

Through the trees they could see a beam of light moving on the beach.

"It's going toward the cove," said Bert excitedly. "Come on! There's no time to waste!"

Keeping his own light off, he led the way to the beach where Sandy used to work. Quietly the children filed into the dark cove. There was no light.

When they reached the brush which hung out over the water, Flossie guided Bert among the branches. He pushed on until he was close to the bluff with enough space to stand up.

He turned on his light and moved forward with the others creeping behind. Suddenly he gasped in surprise. Before him was a wooden door hanging on one hinge.

"It's a ruined boathouse," Nan whispered.

Bert slipped through the doorway onto a catwalk. He flashed the light around. The roof was sagging and the opposite wall of the ancient structure leaned at a crazy angle. But oil stains on the water showed that a boat had been kept here recently.

"There's no other door," Nan said softly. "But there has to be some way to get into the hill, I'm sure."

"Wait here," Bert said quietly.

He walked gingerly over the ancient boards to the back wall of the boathouse. A worn, stained life preserver hung there.

Bert pulled on it gently. With a creak it came forward, bringing a section of the wall with it. He shone his light inside to a brick passage.

"I knew it!" Bert whispered. "Come on!"

He stepped forward just as an unearthly howl came from the tunnel!

CHAPTER XVI

CHOCOLATE PILLOW

THE strange wail died away somewhere inside the hill. Bert shivered in spite of himself.

"Wha-what was that?" Flossie whispered.

"I don't know," said Bert softly, "but I'm going to find out. Is everybody game?"

A soft chorus of "Yes" answered him. Bert moved quietly into the dark passage, beaming his flashlight ahead of him. "Last one in, close the door," he called back softly.

"Okay," said Skip, pulling it shut.

Bert's light showed that the passage forked. The left branch went uphill. The other was level.

As the children hesitated, the loud howl came again from their right. "Help!" cried a voice.

"This way," said Bert.

He headed down the level passage. At the end was a wooden door with an iron ring handle. Bert grasped it and pulled outward.

"Locked!" he whispered.

"But the ring looks old. Maybe we can break it open," Skip suggested. He seized the ring. Placing one foot on the brick wall next to the door, he pulled back as hard as he could. Then he let go with a grunt. "It's giving."

Both boys grabbed the ring and yanked. There was the sound of splintering wood. One more pull and the door came open. Bert aimed his light into the small room.

"Mr. Kruger!" exclaimed Nan as the children hurried inside.

At the same time shrill barking burst out.

"Mop!" Skip cried as the little dog leaped into his arms.

The watchman could hardly believe his eyes. Weakly he thanked his rescuers. In a trembling voice he told the children that someone had knocked him out in the castle. "When I came to, I was in here."

"Do you know who hit you?" Nan asked.

"No," Mr. Kruger replied. "There are three men in the gang and they've been careful not to use any names. But I learned a few things from them."

He told the children that the leader of the gang had worked for the Webb family years before. He knew about the underground passages from the boathouse. "One is a short cut up to the main house. The other leads to this storage room. I've been calling through a tiny barred window that opens in the bluff. But it's so overgrown with brush that nobody can see it from outside.

"Yesterday morning," Mr. Kruger went on, "the red-haired man threw this dog in here." The watchman grinned shakily. "For such a little fellow, he sure set up a big howl. There was a doll blanket and clothes with him," the man added. "They're in the corner."

Bert beamed the light over and Nan picked up the bundle.

"Did the men bring you and Mop some food?" Freddie asked.

"Oh yes, we've had plenty to eat."

Nan asked him, "Did you manage to find out what the men are up to?"

"They've been picking pockets. But what they're really doing is looking for something—I don't know what."

Skip spoke up. "We'd better get out of here now. The park'll be closing soon."

"And maybe the bad men will come back," said Flossie anxiously.

Quietly the children led Mr. Kruger out of the hill and through the cove. When they reached the beach, Happy Island had indeed closed. The lights of the last launch were halfway across the lake.

Just then a large motorboat sped away from

the dock. "There goes Mr. Flotow!" Nan exclaimed in dismay.

"He didn't know we wanted to go home with him," said Bert. "But it's okay. Dad'll come for us as soon as we're missed."

Skip frowned and said, "But first your folks'll call Mr. Flotow to ask about you. I heard him tell Dad he's going to his brother's house. But your parents won't know that. We're stuck for a while."

"Then let's investigate that passage to the main house," said Bert.

Mr. Kruger seated himself on the sand. "I feel kind of shaky," he said. "Suppose I stay here with the dog. Don't be long."

"I'll leave the doll clothes and blanket here," said Nan, placing them beside the watchman.

The five detectives hurried to the secret passage. At the end they faced solid rock.

"Maybe it opens," said Nan.

Bert pushed on it. With a grating noise the big stone pivoted open. He stepped forward cautiously and flashed the light around. He was in a huge empty cellar. Near one end lay two mattresses, one on top of the other.

"What are those for?" Nan whispered.

"I have a hunch," said Bert, remembering the crack he had seen across the slide.

He walked over and aimed his light at the ceiling. A large square section had been cut away, showing the curved underside of the slide. His light picked out the crack and several shiny hinges.

"A trap door!" Nan exclaimed. "So that's how the spooks escaped from the castle!"

"Right," said Bert, then flashed his light along a wall. Against it was a low, sturdy platform with heavy ropes leading to the ceiling. Nearby stood a large motor and a control box with a button on it.

"An elevator," said Skip.

Just then they heard a scraping sound from the other side of the cellar. *The secret entrance was opening!*

Bert snapped off his light and the children froze. They heard stumbling footsteps. The stone grated shut.

Scarcely daring to breathe, Skip and the Bobbseys listened as the newcomers made their way through the pitch darkness. Closer and closer they came!

Suddenly a heavy hand was laid on Bert's arm. "Is that you, Lifty?" a voice growled.

Bert's heart hammered and his mouth was dry. Then an angry voice replied, "I'm here, Ben. If you'd had enough sense to bring your flashlight, you'd know where I am."

The hand was lifted from Bert's arm. "Since you're so smart, why didn't you bring yours?" Ben retorted.

The big stone pivoted open

"I told you. The battery went dead," Lifty replied. "Jim'll be down in a minute with his."

A chill ran through the children. When the leader came with the light, they would be discovered!

Nan felt for the young twins' hands and began to back silently toward the exit. A soft rustle told her that Bert and Skip were doing the same.

Just then a buzzer sounded. "There's the signal," said Ben. "Jim's starting down the slide now."

After several moments the hinged section dropped from the ceiling and the well-dressed man shot down the polished surface. He had his cane under one arm and a big flashlight in his hand. It was turned downward and did not show up the children. As Jim hit the mattresses, the trap door swung silently up again.

"That works great!" said Ben. "Lucky for us I used to be an electronics expert, eh? And a good thing I'm handy with tools!"

"Oh, quit bragging," said Fancy Jim sourly as he stood up.

"But it's neat, boss," the heavy voice protested. "You press the button hidden outside the turret window, start down the slide and the trap door is timed to open just before you get to it."

"Yes, and that's why those Bobbsey kids got hold of my Melrose pen," said Lifty bitterly. "If the trap had opened right away the pen would have come to the cellar when I dropped it."

"All you do is complain," said Ben angrily. "Don't forget I made another way out of this castle too, so we couldn't be trapped."

"Big deal," sneered Fancy Jim. "That elevator was here all the time. The Webbs used it to take things in and out of the cellar. All you did, Ben, was connect up some wires."

"Aw, forget it," Lifty said. "We've still got to find our stuff. I'm sure the builders used that bag somewhere in this crazy fun house. We'll start in the turret again and work down."

The three walked to the low platform and stood on it. Ben kicked the button. The elevator rose slowly with a whirring noise. A panel slid aside in the ceiling and the men disappeared up into the darkness. All was silent.

"Bert, you were right!" Nan whispered excitedly. "It's the Jones gang!"

"Yes," he replied, turning on his light, "and all along they have been looking for something in sand. Now they mention a bag—I'll bet it's a sandbag!"

"But what's in it?" Freddie asked.

"I can guess," said Bert. "The loot from the bank! Those men hid the money in this cellar inside a sandbag."

Skip chuckled. "And when they learned Mr. Flotow was building the castle, they came to pick up the bag, but it was gone!"

"Where could the sandbag be?" Nan asked.

Flossie gave a little gasp of excitement. "Maybe the chocolate pillow on the throne!" she exclaimed. "The pillow's shaped like a bag."

"Let's go see," said Bert quickly. "If the loot's there, we must get it out of the castle before the gang finds it."

He hurried to the elevator and kicked the button. The platform whirred down. He and the girls stood on it and Nan pressed the button with her toe. Skip and Freddie would follow on the next ride.

The elevator rose and stopped in a candy-striped closet. Cautiously Bert opened the door and they stepped into the first-floor room. They had been in the big peppermint wardrobe.

"Look for the elevator button," Bert whispered. "We might need to go down fast." Nan found it inside the closet. It was painted red to match the stripes.

By then Freddie and Skip had come up. Silently the five children went up the spiral staircase and slipped into the throne room. As they hurried to the dais Bert and Skip took out their pocketknives.

While Nan held the light, they cut a long slit in the "chocolate" crust of the pillow. Out came a stream of sand! As Bert shook the bag, dozens of packets of money tumbled to the floor!

Flossie gave a little squeal of excitement.

"Shh!" said Nan sharply.

Quickly the boys put away their knives and started picking up the money.

"Hurry up! Let's get out of here," said Skip anxiously.

While Freddie and Flossie held the bag, the older children stuffed all the bills inside.

"Okay," Bert whispered, "let's go!"

At that moment they were bathed in the glare of a powerful flashlight.

"Drop that bag," barked a voice, "and don't move!"

CHAPTER XVII

HELP!

"RUN! Scatter!" Bert yelled. "I'll go for help."

Instantly the young twins dropped the bag and dashed for the slide.

"Block that!" shouted Fancy Jim. "Don't let 'em get away!"

Bert and Skip ducked under the men's arms and darted through the door.

"Stop!" Jim bellowed and lunged after them.

The boys tore down the spiral stairway, with Ben shouting, "Come back, boss! We don't have a light!"

Fancy Jim paid no attention and went on. Bert and Skip dashed to the wardrobe and slipped inside. They felt for the button. Bert found and pressed it. Down they went!

They reached the cellar and groped through the darkness to the wall. The boys walked along it, pushing on the stones. Finally Skip said, "Here it is!"

As the secret exit swung open, they heard the elevator machinery whirring.

"Somebody's coming," said Bert. "Hurry!"

They ran down the steep, dark passage. Suddenly Fancy Jim's voice echoed through the tunnel. "Stop where you are! You can't get off the island. We'll find you sooner or later!"

The boys raced on. Running footsteps sounded behind them. At the bottom of the tunnel Bert pushed the door leading into the boathouse. *The door did not move!*

"What's the matter?" Skip asked.

"It's stuck or locked!"

The person behind them was coming closer! Together the boys hurled themselves against the door and it flew open. They stumbled into the boathouse. Bert slammed the door behind them. They hastened along the catwalk and outside into the bushes. Minutes later they rounded the curve onto the beach.

"Mr. Kruger's gone!" Bert exclaimed.

Just then the boys heard the crashing of brush in the cove.

"We can't stop now!" said Skip. "Come on!"

The boys ran as fast as they could through the soft sand. A few minutes afterward they reached the pavement. The man was still running behind them. Dodging among rides and booths, the boys made their way through the dark park toward Tiny Town.

Once they stopped to listen. The footsteps were still coming! Bert and Skip hurried past the merry-go-round and crawled under the big plastic cover of the miniature town. They crouched in the darkness, panting.

"I promised I'd get help," Bert whispered.

"But how?" Skip asked. He reminded his friend that there were no boats or telephones. "And we can't use Mr. Flotow's radio. The Administration Building's locked."

Bert gripped Skip's arm as the boys heard the swish of feet moving through the grass. Someone was breathing heavily just outside their hiding place.

The next moment the plastic cover was raised a little and a flashlight beamed partly inside. The gold-headed cane was thrust in. It was moved about for a moment, then withdrawn.

"You're here somewhere," Fancy Jim called harshly. "I'll find you!" The boys heard him move off through the grass.

Bert was very worried about his brother and sisters. Had they been able to escape from the castle? If not, what was happening to them?

Aloud he said, "Skip! Can you really fly your father's plane?"

"Sure, why?"

"We can take up a HELP sign," Bert said excitedly. "Use the one we flew for Mop and just light up the first word."

"You're here somewhere!" Fancy Jim
called harshly

"Great idea!" said Skip. "Let's go!"

Cautiously he lifted the plastic cover and peered out. The moon had risen and the flying field was bathed in white light. No one was in sight.

The boys slipped past the merry-go-round. Keeping to the shadows, they trotted along the Promenade. At the far end they ducked among the trees and started to climb Flyaway Hill.

Halfway up the slope, Bert suddenly whispered, "Listen!" From below came the crackle of twigs.

"Fancy Jim has spotted us!" Skip exclaimed softly.

The boys raced to the top of the hill and sprinted across the field toward the equipment shed. Skip unlocked the door. "Get the sign! It's on top. I'll warm up the plane!"

As he ran off, Bert opened the box and took out the HELP FIND THE DOG MOP sign. Swiftly he unscrewed all the bulbs except those in the word HELP. Then he attached the streamer to the plane. The motor roared.

By now Fancy Jim had run across the moonlit field. He was an arm's length away when Bert started to climb aboard.

"No, you don't!" cried Fancy Jim.

As Bert put one foot into the cockpit, the thief seized the boy's other leg, and struck at him with his cane. Grasping the stick, Bert wrenched it from the man's hand. Then he yanked his leg free and fell into the cockpit.

The plane rolled forward. It taxied down the field with Fancy Jim running behind, waving his fist. The next moment the craft took off.

"When I give you the signal, light up the sign!" Skip yelled.

"Okay!" Bert called.

Below, he could see the castle gleaming in the moonlight. What had happened to Nan, Flossie and Freddie?

As a matter of fact the three children had been playing a game of hide-and-seek in the throne room with Lifty and Ben, who had grabbed Nan's flashlight. But the men were finding it hard to catch the children.

"Grab that boy!" cried Ben, pointing the light at Freddie. The next moment the boy was gone.

"Why didn't you nab him?" Ben bellowed.

"I can't get any of them," complained Lifty. "They jump around like crickets. Why don't you try?"

"I have to stay here and block the slide!" said Ben.

Nan knew the door to the staircase was not far from where the thief stood with his light. She took hold of Freddie's and Flossie's hands and tiptoed toward it. Before they reached the door, the flashlight caught the children.

"Stop them!" Ben roared.

But Lifty was not quick enough. The Bobbseys dashed up the stairs as fast as they could and darted into the royal bed chamber on the next floor.

With Lifty and Ben at their heels, the twins scampered around the big room. The beam of light caught Freddie as he leaped onto the royal bed. Lifty jumped up after him. Freddie let himself down. The trick bed rose into the air and began to swing back and forth.

"Help!" Lifty yelled. "Get me off of this thing!"

Ben, who was again guarding the slide, aimed his light at the bed. The twins saw Lifty stand up, teetering wildly as the bed swung through the air. Yelling, he fell off and hit the floor with a bang.

The next instant the three children ducked through the doorway, but Ben was right behind them. They pounded up the stairs to the turret.

"If only we can make it to the slide," Nan thought, "we can escape!"

But as she reached the top of the stairs, Ben pushed past Freddie and Flossie and barred the door to the turret with his arm.

"Stop right here!" he growled. The twins turned to go down, but Lifty was climbing the stairs toward them.

"Get 'em into that tower room!" he barked to Ben. "I've got a question to ask 'em."

The children were herded into the small, round chamber and lined up next to the window. Ben stood with his back to the slide, waving the flashlight. "Don't get any ideas," he said, "or you'll be sorry. Lifty, go pick up that loot and bring it here."

"Okay," grumbled Lifty and disappeared down the dark stairs. Ben saw Nan glance at the open doorway. "Forget it," he spoke up roughly. "You try to go down and Lifty will nab you at the bottom."

Nan did not reply. The big man chuckled. "We've been keeping an eye on you for some time," he said. "We even rented a car to follow you around. We're too smart to let you get away now."

Nan spoke up boldly. "Lifty followed us home in a motorboat and listened outside our living room window, didn't he?"

"You know too much," Ben growled. "I tried to scare you off by pushing that rock in the cove. Too bad you didn't take the hint!"

"Why did you kidnap Mr. Kruger?" Freddie piped up.

"Because he was too nosy." The man frowned. "Did you find him?"

"Of course," said Nan coolly, then added, "you ought to be sorry for all the bad things you've done."

"We had to look for our loot," Ben replied.

"We even thought it might have been built into that sand pirate." He chuckled. "We didn't miss much. Fancy Jim spotted you kids running down the beach yesterday and was afraid you'd seen him and heard the cane talking. He followed to see where you went. Then he radioed me to meet him in the castle and talk things over."

"We saw you go in," said Flossie.

"Where was Lifty then?" asked Nan.

"In the cellar," said Ben. "He'd been in the boathouse reporting to the boss on his radio."

"Did you invent those little radios?" Freddie asked.

"Sure I did," the man replied boastfully. "We thought of everything. The boss even had a pal in Florida call the Melrose police and give a false report that we were down there."

Just then Lifty appeared in the doorway with the burlap bag of money.

"I heard you, Ben!" he said disgustedly. "What are you doing—telling everything?"

The big man shrugged. "They know so much already, what difference does it make?"

A beam of moonlight showed Lifty's angry face. His eyes narrowed as he looked at the children. "Since they know so much," he said, "they can answer a question for me." He paused. *"What did you do with that ruby?"*

CHAPTER XVIII

IN THE BAG!

"RUBY?" Nan repeated in amazement. "What ruby?" Suddenly she knew. "From Bender's Jewelry Store! You stole it!"

"That's right," Lifty said evenly. "You found it. Now, *where is it?*"

"We don't know," Nan said. The young twins shook their heads earnestly.

"I think they're telling the truth," put in Ben. "Maybe the other ones know—"

"Be quiet!" Lifty said sharply. "I'll handle this." He glared at the twins. "Now you kids start talking!"

Before the children could speak, Ben glanced out the tower window. He gave a gasp of alarm. "Look!"

Sailing through the sky was the word HELP in big, red-lighted letters.

"Who's flying that plane?" Ben cried. "The fellow who owns it left the island."

"It must be Skip!" Nan exclaimed. "Bert told us he knows how."

Lifty groaned. "You Bobbseys have been nothing but trouble!"

"We got to get out!" said Ben anxiously. "That thing can be seen for miles. Every cop in Lakeport will be over here to find out what's the matter."

"I know it," said Lifty sharply. "But what'll we do with these kids?"

"Tie 'em up and slide 'em to the cellar. By the time they're found, we'll be off the island." He pulled a ball of cord from his pocket. "But we can't go without Jim."

"Where is he?" Lifty asked anxiously. "We don't dare wait much longer."

Just then they heard a shout and running footsteps on the tower stairs. The gang leader burst through the doorway. "Cops!" he gasped. "They're coming ashore! Tie up the kids and push 'em down to the cellar!"

"There's no time," protested Lifty, picking up the loot.

"Do what I say!" barked Fancy Jim. "If we let 'em loose, they'll run outside yelling for the police. We'll be nabbed before we get out of the cove!"

"That's right," said Ben. He stepped over to the leader, leaving the chute free.

"Down the slide!" cried Nan, and the twins dived for it.

"Stop!" Lifty yelled, and the men leaped at them.

As the children pulled themselves over the edge, Ben lunged for Freddie. The man lost his balance and fell onto the slide.

"HE-ELP!" he bellowed and grabbed for his companions, who also fell over. Down they all went—thieves, children and the bag of loot. Round and round the curves they whizzed. With a *whoosh* they all spilled into the courtyard!

As they bounced on the foamy rubber, the alarm bell sounded and searchlights were trained on them. Half a dozen policemen ran up and seized the thieves. Officer Lane grabbed the money. As handcuffs were snapped on the three prisoners, the police recognized them.

"A great job, children!" exclaimed Officer Lane. "You've bagged the Jones gang!"

Just then Bert and Skip hurried up. Behind them were Mr. and Mrs. Bobbsey, Mr. Flotow and Phil. The twins' parents hugged their children, and Phil clapped Skip proudly on the back.

"Bert was right about the bank robbers all along," said Mr. Bobbsey, as his son handed the gold-headed cane to one of the policemen.

The prisoners listened grim-faced, while the

Down they went!

twins told what had happened that night. When they finished, Officer Lane spoke up. "There's a reward for the capture of Fancy Jim and his friends, and you twins will get it."

"But we had fun solving the mystery," said Nan. "We didn't do it for money."

"I suggest we give the reward to the children of our sister town in New Zealand," said Bert. The other twins agreed at once.

"I'll give mine, too," said Skip. "After all, you Bobbseys were the real detectives."

Officer Brown picked up the bag of bank loot and turned to Lifty Lemon. "So it was you who stole the ruby, was it? What makes you think the Bobbseys have it?"

Lifty glared at the twins. "I'm not talking," he declared.

Mr. Bobbsey said he and his wife had been very worried. "We had just located Mr. Flotow when Mother saw the HELP sign. We called the police, but they had already seen it and sent a launch to the island. Mr. Flotow brought us out in his motorboat."

"Where's Mop?" Skip asked.

Mr. Bobbsey grinned. "Guarding the boat with Mr. Kruger. Come! We must go."

Ten minutes later the Bobbseys and their friends started for Lakeport. Skip fondled his dog. Mop wriggled happily, then settled down for the ride home. Now and then he gave a soft woof!

"He's happy," said Flossie, resting her head on her mother's shoulder. "Tomorrow we must take Amy her dog," she added sleepily.

The next morning Mrs. Bobbsey telephoned Amy's mother to see if she would take the lonesome dog from the pound. When the answer was yes, she and the twins set off to get it. Then they headed for Cliffside with the big black dog in the back of the station wagon.

The young twins chattered happily. The older ones stared out the window, puzzling over the missing ruby.

"Nan, did you bring Amy's doll clothes and the blanket?" Flossie asked.

Her sister patted the paper bag on the seat beside her. "Here they are." Then suddenly Nan gasped. "The ruby! I think I know where it is!"

"Where?" the others chorused.

"In Amy's little suitcase!"

"How do you figure that?" Bert asked.

Nan reminded the others that on the morning the pendant was stolen they had met Lifty Lemon disguised as an old man. "Right after the police siren blew," she said, "we saw him petting Mop. I believe he had the ruby in his pocket. He was afraid the police might catch him with it. While we were watching the squad car go by, he wound the chain around Mop's neck."

"No wonder Lifty was so eager to get Mop back!" Bert said.

Freddie spoke up excitedly. "But when he got the dog the ruby was gone. That's what the talking cane meant when it said, 'It's not on him.'"

"Of course," said Nan. "But Flossie, you remember what Amy told us about keeping Mop's clothes in the doll's suitcase? She said, 'I didn't let him wear the little necklace.'"

"That's right!" Flossie exclaimed. "She must have found it when she gave him the bath!"

Mrs. Bobbsey smiled. "That's a good theory, Nan. You can prove it in about five minutes."

When they drove up to the Woods' house, Amy was playing on the steps with her suitcase and doll carriage. Her mother was sweeping the porch.

While Mrs. Bobbsey went to explain to Mrs. Wood about the ruby, Amy ran to meet Nan and Flossie. The boys opened the back door of the car. The big black dog jumped out and trotted into the yard.

With a cry, Amy ran over and threw her arms around his neck. "Oh, is he really mine?"

"Yes," Flossie said, beaming.

As Amy squeezed the dog, he licked her face. "Your name's going to be Flopsy," she said to him, "and I'll be your mommy."

"Amy," said Nan quickly, "we brought back your doll clothes." She handed them over. "Put them in your suitcase."

The little girl hurried to the steps. As she opened the bag, everybody crowded around. On a pile of tiny dresses sparkled the ruby pendant!

"This is Mop's," Amy said, picking it up.

"Thank you," said Nan, taking it from her. "It isn't really his, but the man who owns the necklace will be glad to get it back." She handed the ruby to her mother.

"To think I never knew Amy had it," said Mrs. Wood. "I guess it looked like a play necklace to her."

After Amy and her mother had thanked the twins for the dog, the Bobbseys left. On the way home they turned the ruby over to the delighted police chief.

That afternoon the whole family went to Happy Island. "Oh, look!" cried Flossie. Stretched across the Promenade was a huge banner which read:

BOBBSEY DAY

Her mother smiled. "Mr. Flotow has a surprise for you at Tiny Town."

The park owner was waiting for them with the Brewsters and Mop. Both of the other Tiny Town guide teams were there with a crowd of onlookers.

Mop barked and leaped into Flossie's arms. As she cuddled the dog, Mr. Flotow stepped forward.

"Ladies and gentlemen," he said loudly, "you have all heard how the Bobbsey twins caught the bank robbers and rid my island of spooks. Today, in their honor, all rides will be half price!"

The listeners applauded. "From now on, everything on Happy Island will be free to the Bobbseys. And that goes for Skip Brewster, too!"

The embarrassed children beamed happily and thanked Mr. Flotow.

"I thank *you!*" he said warmly. "Business is booming! The capture of the bank robbers was the best publicity I could have had! Now I can go ahead with the swimming pool."

Phil spoke up. "I promised a reward to the person who found Mop. I think Nan and Flossie earned it."

"We ought to have that reward!" said a loud voice. It was Danny. He and Jack pushed up to Phil. "We told 'em where to go for the dog."

"That's true," Nan said to Phil. "You'd better give it to them."

Father and son looked at each other and grinned. "Okay," said Skip. He reached under the ticket table and drew out two big boxes. He opened one carton and lifted out a large doll with blond hair and a pink dress. "Here's yours, Danny," he said, holding out the present to the startled bully.

Meanwhile Phil had taken a pretty blue-dressed doll from the other box. "How about this for you?" he said to Jack.

Everyone laughed. Before the red-faced bullies could leave, Phil added quickly, "We're joking, of course, boys. Come up to Flyaway Hill and I'll give you both a free plane ride."

Just then a cheerful voice called, "I have a surprise for you Bobbseys, too!" It was Sandy, the sand sculptor.

"Are you going to build up Blackbeard again?" Freddie asked eagerly.

Sandy grinned. "No! He's nothing but an old pirate! I'm going to make statues of four great detectives." He winked at Flossie. "And I'll bet you can guess who they are!"